INTRODUCING. . .

Kate Allfield—a luscious jewel thief with a knack for hiding her booty in the oddest (and most interesting) places. . .

Major Smart—an unscrupulous landlord, often caught red-handed in an innocent lady's apartment. . .

"Broads" Tillson—Chicago hood and strong-arm enforcer, who got his nickname from the way he made his living. . .

Simon Templar takes on all three, and finds himself in a hotbed of deadly but delightful intrigue.

Don't miss other Ace Charter titles in the Saint series:

THE SAINT ABROAD
THE SAINT AND THE PEOPLE IMPORTERS
VENDETTA FOR THE SAINT
CATCH THE SAINT
THE SAINT AND THE HAPSBURG
  NECKLACE
THE AVENGING SAINT
ALIAS THE SAINT
FEATURING THE SAINT
THE SAINT AT THE THIEVES' PICNIC
THE SAINT VS. SCOTLAND YARD
THE SAINT IN ACTION
THE SAINT INTERVENES
THE SAINT ON THE SPANISH MAIN
THE SAINT ERRANT
THE SAINT AND THE SIZZLING
  SABOTEUR
CALL FOR THE SAINT
THE SAINT OVERBOARD
THE SAINT AND THE HAPPY
  HIGHWAYMAN

LESLIE CHARTERIS

the Saint

THE SAINT—
THE BRIGHTER
BUCCANEER

CHARTER
NEW YORK

A Division of Charter Communications Inc.
A GROSSET & DUNLAP COMPANY
51 Madison Avenue
New York, New York 10010

THE SAINT—THE BRIGHTER BUCCANEER
Copyright ©1932, 1933, by Leslie Charteris.

An Ace Charter Book
by arrangement with Doubleday and Company, Inc.

First Ace Charter Printing: August 1981
Published simultaneously in Canada

2 4 6 8 0 9 7 5 3 1
Manufactured in the United States of America

Contents

The Brain Workers...1
The Export Trade..16
The Tough Egg..29
The Bad Baron..45
The Brass Buddha...61
The Perfect Crime..79
The Unpopular Landlord..............................95
The New Swindle...114
The Five Thousand Pound Kiss.....................131
The Blind Spot..151
The Unusual Ending......................................168

THE BRAIN WORKERS

"Happy" Fred Jorman was a man with a griev-
ance. He came to his partner with a tale of woe.

"It was just an ordinary bit of business, Meyer.
I met him in the Alexandra—he seemed interested
in horses, and he looked so lovely and innocent.
When I told him about the special job I'd got for
Newmarket that afternoon, and it came to suggest-
ing he might like to put a bit on himself, I'd hardly
got the words out of my mouth before he was
pushing a tenner across the table. Well, after I'd
been to the 'phone I told him he'd got a three-to-
one winner, and he was so pleased he almost wept
on my shoulder. And I paid him out in cash. That
was thirty pounds—thirty real pounds he had off
me—but I wasn't worrying. I could see I was going
to clean him out. He was looking at the notes I'd
given him as if he was watching all his dreams
come true. And that was when I bought him another drink and started telling him about the real big
job of the day. 'It's honestly not right for me to be
letting you in at all,' I said, 'but it gives me a lot of
pleasure to see a young sport like you winning
some money,' I said. 'This horse I'm talking about
now,' I said, 'could go twice around the course

1

while all the other crocks were just beginning to realise that the race had started; but I'll eat my hat if it starts at a fraction less than five to one,' I said."

"Well?"

"Well, the mug looked over his roll and said he'd only got about a hundred pounds, including what he'd won already, and that didn't seem enough to put on a five-to-one certainty. 'But if you'll excuse me a minute while I go to my bank, which is just round the corner,' he said, 'I'll give you five hundred pounds to put on for me.' And off he went to get the money—"

"And never came back," said the smaller speaking part, with the air of a Senior Wrangler solving the first problem in a child's book of arithmetic.

"That's just it, Meyer," said Happy Fred aggrievedly. "He never came back. He stole thirty pounds off me, that's what it amounts to—he ran away with the ground-bait I'd given him, and wasted the whole of my afternoon, not to mention all the brain-work I'd put into spinning him the yarn—"

"Brain work!" said Meyer.

Simon Templar would have given much to overhear that conversation. It was his one regret that he never had the additional pleasure of knowing exactly what his pigeons said when they woke up and found themselves bald.

Otherwise, he had very few complaints to make about the way his thirty years of energetic life had treated him. "Do others as they would do you," was his motto; and for several years past he had carried out the injunction with a simple and unswerving whole-heartedness, to his own continual entertainment and profit. "There are," said the Saint, "less interesting ways of spending wet week-ends. . . ."

Certainly it was a wet week-end when he met Ruth Eden, though he happened to be driving home along that lonely stretch of the Windsor road after a strictly lawful occasion.

To her, at first, he was only the providential man in the glistening leather coat who came striding across from the big open Hirondel that had skidded to a standstill a few yards away. She had seen his lights whizzing up behind them, and had managed to put her foot through the window as he went past—Mr. Julian Lamantia was too strong for her, and she was thoroughly frightened. The man in the leather coat twitched open the nearest door of the limousine and propped himself gracefully against it, with the broken glass crunching under his feet. His voice drawled pleasantly through the hissing rain.

"Evening, madam. This is Knight Errants Unlimited. Anything we can do?"

"If you're going towards London," said the girl quickly, "could you give me a lift?"

The man laughed. It was a short, soft lilt of a laugh that somehow made the godsend of his arrival seem almost too good to be true.

An arm sheathed in wet sheepskin shot into the limousine—and Mr. Lamantia shot out. The feat of muscular prestidigitation was performed so swiftly and slickly that she took a second or two to absorb the fact that it had indubitably eventuated and travelled on into the past tense. By which time Mr. Lamantia was picking himself up out of the mud, with the rain spotting the dry portions of his very natty check suiting and his vocabulary functioning on full throttle.

He stated, amongst other matters, that he would teach the intruder to mind his own unmentionable business; and the intruder smiled almost lazily.

"We don't like you," said the intruder.

He ducked comfortably under the wild swing that Mr. Lamantia launched at him, collared the raving man below the hips, and hoisted him, kicking and struggling, on to one shoulder. In this manner they disappeared from view. Presently there was a loud splash from the river bank a few yards away, and the stranger returned alone.

"Can your friend swim?" he inquired interestedly.

The girl stepped out into the road, feeling rather at a loss for any suitable remark. Somewhere in the damp darkness Mr. Lamantia was demonstrating a fluency of discourse which proved that he was contriving to keep at least his mouth above water; and the conversational powers of her rescuer showed themselves to be, in their own way, equally superior to any awe of circumstances.

As he led her across to his own car he talked with a charming lack of embarrassment.

"Over on our left we have the island of Runnymede, where King John signed the Magna Carta in the year 1215. It is by virtue of this Great Charter that Englishmen have always enjoyed complete freedom to do everything that they are not forbidden to do. . . ."

The Hirondel was humming on towards London at a smooth seventy miles an hour before she was able to utter her thanks.

"I really was awfully relieved when you came along—though I'm afraid you've lost me my job."

"Like that, was it?"

"I'm afraid so. If you happen to know a nice man who wants an efficient secretary for purely secretarial purposes, I could owe you even more than I do now."

It was extraordinarily easy to talk to him—she was not quite sure why. In some subtle way he succeeded in weaving over her a fascination that was unique in her experience. Before they were in London she had outlined to him the whole story of her life. It was not until afterwards that she began to wonder how on earth she had ever been able to imagine that a perfect stranger could be interested in the recital of her inconsiderable affairs. For the tale she had to tell was very ordinary—a simple sequence of family misfortunes which had forced her into a profession amongst whose employers the Lamantias are not so rare that any museum has yet thought it worth while to include a stuffed specimen in the catalogue of its exhibits.

"And then, when my father died, my mother seemed to go a bit funny, poor darling! Anyone with a get-rich-quick scheme could take money off her. She ended up by meeting a man who was selling some wonderful shares that were going to multiply their value by ten in a few months. She gave him everything we had left; and a week or two later we found that the shares weren't worth the paper they were printed on."

"And so you joined the world's workers?"

She laughed softly.

"The trouble is to make anyone believe I really

want to work. I'm rather pretty, you know, when you see me properly. I seem to put ideas into middle-aged heads."

She was led on to tell him so much about herself that they had reached her address in Bloomsbury before she remembered that she had not even asked him his name.

"Templar—Simon Templar," he said gently.

She was in the act of fitting her key into the front door, and she was so startled that she turned round and stared at him, half doubtful whether she ought to laugh.

But the man in the leather coat was not laughing, though a little smile was flickering round his mouth. The light over the door picked out the clean-cut buccaneering lines of his face under the wide-brimmed filibuster's hat, and glinted back from the incredibly blue eyes in such a blaze of merry mockery as she had never seen before. . . . It dawned upon her, against all her ideas of probability, that he wasn't pulling her leg. . . .

"Do you mean that I've really met the Saint?" she asked dizzily.

"That's so. The address is in the telephone book. If there's anything else I can do, any time—"

"Angels and ministers of grace!" said the girl weakly, and left him standing there alone on the steps; and Simon Templar went laughing back to his car.

He came home feeling as pleased as if he had won three major wars single-handed, for the Saint made for himself an atmosphere in which no adventure could be commonplace. He pitched his hat into a corner, swung himself over the table, and kissed the hands of the tall, slim girl who rose to meet him.

"Pat, I have rescued the most beautiful damsel, and I have thrown a man named Julian Lamantia into the Thames. Does life hold any more?"

"There's mud on your face, and you're as wet as if you'd been in the river yourself," said his lady.

The Saint had the priceless gift of not asking too much of life. He cast his bread with joyous lavishness upon the waters, and tranquilly assumed that he would find it after many days—buttered and thickly spread with jam. In his philosophy that night's adventure was sufficient unto itself; and when, twenty-four hours later, his fertile brain was plunged deep into a new interest that had come to him, he would probably have forgotten Ruth Eden altogether, if she had not undoubtedly recognised his name. The Saint had his own vanity.

Consequently, when she rang up one afternoon and announced that she was coming to see him, he was not utterly dumbfounded.

She arrived about six o'clock, and he met her on the doorstep with a cocktail shaker in his hand.

"I'm afraid I left you very abruptly the other night," she said. "You see, I'd read all about you in the newspapers, and it was rather overpowering to find that I'd been talking to the Saint for three-quarters of an hour without knowing it. In fact, I was very rude; and I think it's awfully sweet of you to have me."

"I think it's awfully sweet of you to be had," said Simon gravely. "Do you like it with a dash?"

He sat her down with a dry Martini and a cigarette, and once again she felt the strange sense of confidence that he inspired. It was easier to broach the object of her visit than she had expected.

"I was looking through some old papers yesterday, and I happened to come across those shares I was telling you about—the last lot my mother bought. I suppose it was ridiculous of me to think of coming to you, but it occurred to me that you'd be the very man who'd know what I ought to do about them—if there is anything that can be done. I've got quite a lot of cheek," she said, smiling.

Simon slipped the papers out of the envelope she handed him and glanced over them. There were ten of them, and each one purported to be a certificate attributing to the bearer two hundred £1 shares in the British Honduras Mineral Development Trust.

"If they're only worth the paper they're printed on, even that ought to be something," said the Saint. "The engraving is really very artistic."

He gazed at the shares sadly. Then, with a shrug, he replaced them in the envelope and smiled.

"May I keep them for a day or two?"

She nodded.

"I'd be frightfully grateful." She was watching him with a blend of amusement and curiosity; and then she laughed. "Excuse me staring at you like this, but I've never met a desperate criminal before. And you really are the Saint—you go about killing dope traffickers and swindling swindlers and all that sort of thing?"

"And that sort of thing," admitted the Saint mildly.

"But how do you find them? I mean, if I had to go out and find a swindler, for instance—"

"You've met one already. Your late employer

runs the J. L. Investment Bureau, doesn't he? I can't say I know much about his business, but I should be very surprised if any of his clients made their fortunes through acting on his advice."

She laughed.

"I can't think of any who have done so; but even when you've found your man—"

"Well, every case is taken on its merits; there's no formula. Now, did you ever hear what happened to a bloke named Francis Lemuel—"

He amused her for an hour with the recital of some of his more entertaining misdeeds; and when she left she was still wondering why his sins seemed so different in his presence, and why it was so impossible to feel virtuously shocked by all that he admitted he had done.

During the next few days, he gave a considerable amount of thought to the problem of the Eden family's unprofitable investments; and since he had never been afflicted with doubts of his own remarkable genius, he was not surprised when the course of his inquiries produced a possible market which had nothing at all to do with the Stock Exchange. Simon had never considered the Stock Exchange, anyway.

He was paying particular attention to the correctly rakish angle of his hat preparatory to sallying forth on a certain morning when the front door bell rang and he went to open to the visitor. A tall, saturnine man with white moustache and bushy white eyebrows stood on the mat, and it is an immutable fact of this chronicle that he was there by appointment.

"Can I see Captain Tombs? My name—"

"Is Wilmer-Steak?"

"Steck."

"Steck. Pleased to meet you. I'm Captain
Tombs. Step in, comrade. How are you off for
time?"

Mr. Wilmer-Steck suffered himself to be pro-
pelled into the sitting-room, where he consulted a
massive gold watch.

"I think I shall have plenty of time to conclude
our business, if you have enough time to do your
share," he said.

"I mean, do you think you could manage to wait
a few minutes? Make yourself at home till I come
back?" With a bewildering dexterity the Saint shot
cigarette-box, matches, pile of magazines, decanter, and siphon on to the table in front of the
visitor. "Point is, I absolutely must dash out and
see a friend of mine. I can promise not to be more
than fifteen minutes. Could you possibly wait?"

Mr. Wilmer-Steck blinked.

"Why, certainly, if the matter is urgent, Captain
—er—"

"Tombs. Help yourself to anything you want.
Thanks so much. Pleased to see you. Bye-bye."
said the Saint.

Mr. Wilmer-Steck felt himself wrung warmly by
the hand, heard the sitting-room door bang, heard
the front door bang, and saw the figure of his host
flying past the open windows; and he was left pardonably breathless.

After a time, however, he recovered sufficiently
to help himself to a whisky and soda and a
cigarette, and he was sipping and puffing appreciatively when the telephone began to ring.

He frowned at it vaguely for a few seconds; and
then he realised that he must be alone in the house,

for no one came to take the call. After some further hesitation, he picked up the receiver.

"Hullo," he said.

"Listen, Simon—I've got great news for you," said the wire. "Remember those shares of yours you were asking me to make inquiries about? Well, it's quite true they were worth nothing yesterday, but they'll be worth anything you like to ask for them to-morrow. Strictly confidential till they release the news, of course, but there isn't a doubt it's true. Your company has struck one of the biggest gushers on earth—it's spraying the landscape for miles around. The papers'll be full of it in twenty-four hours. You're going to pick up a fortune!"

"Oh!" said Mr. Wilmer-Steck.

"Sorry I can't stop to tell you more now, laddie," said the man on the wire. "I've got a couple of important clients waiting, and I must see them. Suppose we meet for a drink later. Berkeley at six, what?"

"Ah," said Mr. Wilmer-Steck.

"Right-ho, then, you lucky old devil. So long!"

"So long," said Mr. Wilmer-Steck.

He replaced the receiver carefully on its bracket, and it was not until several minutes afterwards that he noticed that his cigarette had gone out.

Then, depositing it fastidiously in the fireplace and helping himself to a fresh one, he turned to the telephone again and dialed a number.

He had scarcely finished his conversation when the Saint erupted volcanically back into the house; and Mr. Wilmer-Steck was suffering from such profound emotion that he plunged into the subject of his visit without preamble.

"Our directors have gone carefully into the matter of those shares you mentioned, Captain Tombs, and I am happy to be able to tell you that we are prepared to buy them immediately, if we can come to an agreement. By the way, will you tell me again the exact extent of your holding?"

"A nominal value of two thousand pounds," said the Saint. "But as for their present value—"

"Two thousand pounds!" Mr. Wilmer-Steck rolled the words almost gluttonously round his tongue. "And I don't think you even told us the name of the company."

"The British Honduras Mineral Development Trust."

"Ah, yes! The British Honduras Mineral Development Trust! . . . Naturally our position must seem somewhat eccentric to you, Captain Tombs," said Mr. Wilmer-Steck, who appeared to have only just become conscious of the fact, "but I can assure you—"

"Don't bother," said the Saint briefly.

He went to his desk and flicked open a drawer, from which he extracted the bundle of shares.

"I know your position as well as you know it yourself. It's one of the disadvantages of running a bucket-shop that you have to have shares to work on. You couldn't have anything more worthless than this bunch, so I'm sure everyone will be perfectly happy. Except, perhaps, your clients—but we don't have to worry about them, do we?"

Mr. Wilmer-Steck endeavoured to look pained, but his heart was not in the job.

"Now, if you sold those shares for, say, three hundred pounds—"

"Or supposing I got five hundred for them—"

"If you were offered four hundred pounds, for instance—"

"And finally accepted five hundred—"

"If, as we were saying, you accepted five hundred pounds," agreed Mr. Wilmer-Steck, conceding the point reluctantly, "I'm sure you would not feel you had been unfairly treated."

"I should try to conceal my grief," said the Saint.

He thought that his visitor appeared somewhat agitated, but he never considered the symptom seriously. There was a little further argument before Mr. Wilmer-Steck was persuaded to pay over the amount in cash. Simon counted out the fifty crisp new ten-pound notes which came to him across the table, and passed the share certificates over in exchange. Mr. Wilmer-Steck counted and examined them in the same way.

"I suppose you're quite satisfied?" said the Saint. "I've warned you that to the best of my knowledge and belief those shares aren't worth a fraction of the price you've paid for them—"

"I am perfectly satisfied," said Mr. Wilmer-Steck. He pulled out his large gold chronometer and glanced at the dial. "And now, if you will excuse me, my dear Captain Tombs. I find I am already late for an important engagement."

He made his exit with almost indecent haste.

In an office overlooking the Haymarket he found two men impatiently awaiting his return. He took off his hat, mopped his forehead, ran a hand over his waistcoat, and gasped.

"I've lost my watch," he said.

"Damn your watch," said Mr. Julian Lamantia

callously. "Have you got those shares?"

"My pocket must have been picked," said the bereaved man plaintively. "Yes, I got the shares. Here they are. It was a wonderful watch, too. And don't you forget I'm on to half of everything we make."

Mr. Lamantia spread out the certificates in front of him, and the man in the brown bowler who was perched on a corner of the desk leaned over to look.

It was the latter who spoke first.

"Are these the shares you bought, Meyer?" he asked in a hushed whisper.

"Wilmer-Steck" nodded vigorously.

"They're going to make a fortune for us. Gushers blowing oil two hundred yards in the air— that's the news you'll see in the papers to-morrow. I've never worked so hard and fast in my life, getting Tombs to—"

"*Who?*" asked the brown bowler huskily.

"Captain Tombs—the mug I was working. But it's brain that does it, as I'm always saying. . . . What's the matter with you, Fred—are you feeling ill?"

Mr. Julian Lamantia swivelled round in his chair.

"Do you know anything about these shares, Jorman?" he demanded.

The brown bowler swallowed.

"I ought to," he said. "I was doing a big trade in them three or four years ago. And that damned fool has paid five hundred pounds of our money for 'em—to the same man that swindled me of thirty pounds only last week! There never was a British Honduras Mineral Development Trust till I invented it and printed the shares myself. And that—that—"

Meyer leaned feebly on the desk.

"But listen, Fred," he pleaded. "Isn't there some mistake? You can't mean—After all the imagination and brain work I put into getting those—shares—"

"Brain work!" snarled Happy Fred.

THE EXPORT TRADE

It is a notable fact, which might be made the subject of a profound philosophical discourse by anyone with time to spare for these recreations, that the characteristics which go to make a successful buccaneer are almost the same as those required by the detective whose job it is to catch him.

That he must be a man of inifinite wit and resource goes without saying; but there are other and more uncommon essentials. He must have an unlimited memory not only for faces and names, but also for every odd and out-of-the-way fact that comes to his knowledge. Out of a molehill of coincidence he must be able to build up a mountain of inductive speculation that would make Sherlock Holmes feel dizzy. He must be a man of infinite human sympathy, with an unstinted gift for forming weird and wonderful friendships. He must, in fact, be equally like the talented historian whose job it is to chronicle his exploits—with the outstanding difference that instead of being free to ponder the problems which arise in the course of his vocation for sixty hours, his decisions will probably have to be formed in sixty seconds.

Simon Templar fulfilled at least one of these

qualifications to the *n*th degree. He had queer friends dotted about in every outlandish corner of the globe, and if many of them lived in unromantic-sounding parts of London, it was not his fault. Strangely enough, there were not many of them who knew that the debonair young man with the lean, tanned face and gay blue eyes who drifted in and out of their lives at irregular intervals was the notorious law-breaker known to everyone as the Saint. Certainly old Charlie Milton did not know.

The Saint, being in the regions of the Tottenham Court Road one afternoon with half an hour to dispose of, dropped into Charlie's attic work-room and listened to a new angle of the industrial depression.

"There's not much doing in my line these days," said Charlie, wiping his steel-rimmed spectacles. "When nobody's going in for real expensive jewellery, it stands to reason they don't need any dummies. Look at this thing—the first big bit of work I've had for weeks."

He produced a glittering rope of diamonds, set in a cunning chain of antique silver and ending in a wonderfully elaborate heart-shaped pendant. The sight of it should have made any honest buccaneer's mouth water, but it so happened that Simon Templar knew better. For that was the secret of Charlie Milton's employment.

Up there in his dingy little shop he laboured with marvellously delicate craftsmanship over the imitations which had made his name known to every jeweller in London. Sometimes there were a hundred thousand pounds' worth of precious stones littered over his bench, and he worked under the

watchful eye of a detective detailed to guard them.
Whenever a piece of jewellery was considered too
valuable to be displayed by its owner on ordinary
occasions, it was sent to Charlie Milton for him to
make one of his amazingly exact facsimiles; and
there was many a wealthy dowager who brazenly
paraded Charlie's handiwork at minor social func-
tions, while the priceless originals were safely
stored in a safe deposit.

"The Kellman necklace," Charlie explained toss-
ing it carelessly back into a drawer. "Lord Palfrey
ordered it from me a month ago, and I was just
finishing it when he went bankrupt. I had twenty-
five pounds advance when I took it on, and I expect that's all I shall see for my trouble. The
necklace is being sold with the rest of his things,
and how do I know whether the people who buy it
will want my copy?"

It was not an unusual kind of conversation to
find its place in the Saint's varied experience, and
he never foresaw the part it was to play in his career. Some days later he happened to notice a
newspaper paragraph referring to the sale of Lord
Palfrey's house and effects; but he thought nothing
more of the matter, for men like Lord Palfrey were
not Simon Templar's game.

In the days when some fresh episode of Saintly
audacity was one of the most dependable weekly
stand-bys of the daily press, the victims of his lawlessness had always been men whose reputations
would have emerged considerably dishevelled from
such a searching inquiry as they were habitually at
pains to avoid; and although the circumstances of
Simon Templar's life had altered a great deal since
then, his elastic principles of morality performed

their acrobatic contortions within much the same limits.

That those circumstances should have altered at all was not his choice; but there are boundaries which every buccaneer must eventually reach, and Simon Templar had reached them rather rapidly. The manner of his reaching them has been related elsewhere, and there were not a few people in England who remembered that story. For one week of blazing hadlines the secret of the Saint's real identity had been published up and down the country for all to read; and although there were many to whom the memory had grown dim, and who could still describe him only by the nickname which he had made famous, there were many others who had not forgotten. The change had its disadvantages, for one of the organisations which would never forget had its headquarters at Scotland Yard; but there were occasional compensations in the strange commissions which sometimes came the Saint's way.

One of these arrived on a day in June, brought by a sombrely dressed man who called at the flat on Piccadilly where Simon Templar had taken up his temporary abode—the Saint was continually changing his address, and this palatial apartment with tall windows overlooking the Green Park was his latest fancy. The visitor was an elderly white-haired gentleman with the understanding eyes and air of tremendous discretion which one associates in imagination with the classical type of family solicitor, and it was a solicitor that he immediately confessed himself to be.

"To put it as briefly as possible, Mr. Templar," he said, "I am authorised to ask if you would undertake to deliver a sealed package to an address in

Paris which will be given you. All your expenses will be paid, of course; and you will be offered a fee of one hundred pounds."

Simon lighted a cigarette and blew a cloud of smoke at the ceiling.

"It sounds easy enough," he remarked. "Would it not be cheaper to send it by post?"

"That package, Mr. Templar—the contents of which I am not allowed to disclose—is insured for five thousand pounds," said the solicitor impressively. "But I fear that four times that sum would not compensate for the loss of an article which is the only thing of its kind in the world. The ordinary detective agencies have already been considered, but our client feels that they are scarcely competent to deal with such an important task. We have been warned that an attempt may be made to steal the package, and it is our client's wish that we should endeavour to secure the services of your own—ah—singular experience."

The Saint thought it over. He knew that the trade in illicit drugs does not go on to any appreciable extent from England to the Continent, but rather in the reverse direction; and apart from such a possibility as that the commission seemed straightforward enough.

"Your faith in my reformed character is almost touching," said the Saint at length; and the solicitor smiled faintly.

"We are relying on the popular estimate of your sporting instincts."

"When do you want me to go?"

The solicitor placed the tips of his fingers together with a discreet modicum of satisfaction.

"I take it that you are prepared to accept our offer?"

"I don't see why I shouldn't. A pal of mine who came over the other day told me there was a darn good show at the Folies Bergère, and since you're only young once—"

"Doubtless you will be permitted to include the entertainment in your bill of expenses," said the solicitor dryly. "If the notice is not too short, we should be very pleased if you were free to visit the —ah—Folies Bergère to-morrow night."

"Suits me," murmured the Saint laconically.

The solicitor rose.

"You will travel by air, of course," he said. "I shall return later this evening to deliver the package into your keeping, after which you will be solely responsible. If I might give you a hint, Mr. Templar," he added, as the Saint shepherded him to the door, "you will take particular pains to conceal it while you are travelling. It has been suggested to us that the French police are not incorruptible."

He repeated his warning when he came back at six o'clock and left Simon with a brown-paper packet about four inches square and two inches deep, in which the outlines of a stout cardboard box could be felt. Simon weighed the package several times in his hand—it was neither particularly light nor particularly heavy, and he puzzled over its possible contents for some time. The address to which it was to be delivered was typed on a plain sheet of paper; Simon committed it to memory, and burnt it.

Curiosity was the Saint's weakness. It was that

same insatiable curiosity which had made his fortune, for he was incapable of looking for long at
anything that struck him as being the least bit
peculiar without succumbing to the temptation to
probe deeper into its peculiarities. It never entered
his head to betray the confidence that had been
placed in him, so far as the safety of the package
was concerned; but the mystery of its contents was
one which he considered had a definite bearing on
whatever risks he had agreed to take. He fought off
his curiosity until he got up the next morning, and
then it got the better of him. He opened the packet
after his early breakfast, carefully removing the
seals intact with a hot palette-knife, and was very
glad that he had done so.

When he drove down to Croydon aerodrome later the package had been just as carefully re-
fastened, and no one would have known that it had
been opened. He carried it inside a book, from
which he had cut the printed part of the pages to
leave a square cavity encircled by the margins; and
he was prepared for trouble.

He checked in his suitcase and waited around
patiently during the dilatory system of prepara-
tions which for some extraordinary reason is introduced to negative the theoretical speed of air trans-
port. He was fishing out his cigarette-case for the
second time when a dark and strikingly pretty girl,
who had been waiting with equal patience, came
over and asked him for a light.

Simon produced his lighter, and the girl took a
packet of cigarettes from her bag and offered him
one.

"Do they always take as long as this?" she asked.

"Always when I'm travelling," said the Saint resignedly. "Another thing I should like to know is why they have to arrange their time-tables so that you never have the chance to get a decent lunch. Is it for the benefit of the French restaurants at dinnertime?"

She laughed.

"Are we fellow passengers?"

"I don't know. I'm for Paris."

"I'm for Ostend."

The Saint sighed.

"Couldn't you change your mind and come to Paris?"

He had taken one puff from the cigarette. Now he took a second, while she eyed him impudently. The smoke had an unfamiliar, slightly bitter taste to it. Simon drew on the cigarette again thoughtfully, but this time he held the smoke in his mouth and let it trickle out again presently, as if he had inhaled. The expression on his face never altered, although the last thing he had expected had been trouble of that sort.

"Do you think we could take a walk outside?" said the girl. "I'm simply stifling."

"I think it might be a good idea," said the Saint.

He walked out with her into the clear morning sunshine, and they strolled idly along the gravel drive. The rate of exchange had done a great deal to discourage foreign travel that year, and the air port was unusually deserted. A couple of men were climbing out of a car that had drawn up beside the building; but apart from them there was only one other car turning in at the gates leading from the main road, and a couple of mechanics fussing round a gigantic Handley-Page that was ticking over on the tarmac.

"Why did you give me a doped cigarette?" asked the Saint with perfect casualness; but as the girl turned and stared at him his eyes leapt to hers with the cold suddenness of bared steel.

"I—I don't understand. Do you mind telling me what you mean?"

Simon dropped the cigarette and trod on it deliberately.

"Sister," he said, "if you're thinking of a Simon Templar who was born yesterday, let me tell you it was someone else of the same name. You know, I was playing that cigarette trick before you cut your teeth."

The girl's hand went to her mouth; then it went up in a kind of wave. For a moment the Saint was perplexed; and then he started to turn. She was looking at something over his shoulder, but his head had not revolved far enough to see what it was before the solid weight of a sandbag slugged viciously into the back of his neck. He had one instant of feeling his limbs sagging powerlessly under him, while the book he carried dropped from his hand and sprawled open to the ground; and then everything went dark.

He came back to earth in a small barely furnished office overlooking the landing-field, and in the face that was bending over him he recognised the round pink countenance of Chief Inspector Teal, of Scotland Yard.

"Were you the author of that clout?" he demanded, rubbing the base of his skull tenderly. "I didn't think you could be so rough."

"I didn't do it," said the detective shortly. "But we've got the man who did—if you want to charge him. I thought you'd have known Kate Allfield, Saint."

Simon looked at him.

"What—not 'the Mug'? I have heard of her, but this is the first time we've met. And she nearly made me smoke a sleepy cigarette!" He grimaced. "What was the idea?"

"That's what we're waiting for you to tell us," said Teal grimly. "We drove in just as they knocked you out. We know what they were after all right—the Deacon's gang beat them to the necklace, but that wouldn't make the Green Cross bunch give up. What I want to know is when you started working with the Deacon."

"This is right over my head," said the Saint, just as bluntly. "Who is this Deacon, and who the hell are the Green Cross bunch?"

Teal faced him calmly.

"The Green Cross bunch are the ones that slugged you. The Deacon is the head of the gang that got away with the Palfrey jewels yesterday. He came to see you twice yesterday afternoon—we got the wire that he was planning a big job and we were keeping him under observation, but the jewels weren't missed till this morning. Now I'll hear what you've got to say; but before you begin I'd better warn you—"

"Wait a minute." Simon took out his cigarette-case and helped himself to a smoke. "With an unfortunate reputation like mine, I expect it'll take me some time to drive it into your head that I don't know a thing about the Deacon. He came to me yesterday and said he was a solicitor—he wanted me to look after a valuable sealed packet that he was sending over to Paris, and I took on the job. That's all. He wouldn't even tell me what was in it."

"Oh, yes?" The detective was dangerously polite. "Then I suppose it'd give you the surprise of your life if I told you that package you were carrying contained a diamond necklace valued at about eight thousand pounds?"

"It would," said the Saint.

Teal turned.

There was a plain-clothes man standing guard by the door, and on the table in the middle of the room was a litter of brown paper and tissue in the midst of which gleamed a small heap of coruscating stones and shining metal. Teal put a hand to the heap of jewels and lifted it up into a streamer of iridescent fire.

"This is it," he said.

"May I have a look at it?" said the Saint.

He took the necklace from Teal's hand and studied it closely under the light. Then he handed it back with a brief grin.

"If you could get eighty pounds for it, you'd be lucky," he said. "It's a very good imitation, but I'm afraid the stones are only jargoons."

The detective's eyes went wide. Then he snatched the necklace away and examined it himself.

He turned round again slowly.

"I'll begin to believe you were telling the truth for once, Templar," he said, and his manner had changed so much that the effect would have been comical without the back-handed apology. "What do you make of it?"

"I think we've both been had;" said the Saint. "After what you've told me, I should think the

Deacon knew you were watching him, and knew he'd have to get the jewels out of the country in a hurry. He could probably fence most of them quickly, but no one would touch that necklace—it's too well known. He had the rather artistic idea of trying to get me to do the job—"

"Then why should he give you a fake?"

Simon shrugged.

"Maybe that Deacon is smoother than any of us thought. My God, Teal—think of it! Suppose even all this was just a blind—for you to know he'd been to see me—for you to get after me as soon as the jewels were missed—hear I'd left for Paris—chase me to Croydon—and all the time the real necklace is slipping out by another route—"

"God damn!" said Chief Inspector Teal, and launched himself at the telephone with surprising speed for such a portly and lethargic man.

The plain-clothes man at the door stood aside almost respectfully for the Saint to pass.

Simon fitted his hat on rakishly and sauntered out with his old elegance. Out in the waiting-room an attendant was shouting, "All Ostend and Brussels passengers, please!"—and outside on the tarmac a roaring aeroplane was warming up its engines. Simon Templar suddenly changed his mind about his destination.

"I will give you thirty thousand guilders for the necklace," said Van Roeper, the little Jew of Amsterdam to whom the Saint went with his booty.

"I'll take fifty thousand," said the Saint; and he got it.

He fulfilled another of the qualifications of a successful buccaneer, for he never forgot a face. He had had a vague idea from the first that he had seen the Deacon somewhere before, but it had not been until that morning, when he woke up, that he had been able to place the amiable solicitor who had been so anxious to enlist his dubious services; and he felt that fortune was very kind to him.

Old Charlie Milton, who had been dragged away from his breakfast to sell him the facsimile for eighty pounds, felt much the same.

THE TOUGH EGG

Chief Inspector Teal caught Larry the Stick at Newcastle as he was trying to board an outward-bound Swedish timber ship. He did not find the five thousand pounds worth of bonds and jewellery which Larry took from the Temple Lane Safe Deposit; but it may truthfully be reported that no one was more surprised about that than Larry himself.

They broke open the battered leather suitcase to which Larry was clinging as affectionately as if it contained the keys of the Bank of England, and found in it a cardboard box which was packed to bursting point with what must have been one of the finest collections of small pebbles and old newspapers to which any burglar had ever attached himself; and Larry stared at it with glazed and incredulous eyes.

"Is one of you busies saving up for a rainy day?" he demanded, when he could speak; and Mr. Teal was not amused.

"No one's been to that bag except when you saw us open it," he said shortly. "Come on, Larry—

let's hear where you hid the stuff."

"I didn't hide it," said Larry flatly. He was prepared to say more, but suddenly he shut his mouth. He could be an immensely philosophic man when there was nothing left for him to do except to be philosophic, and one of his major problems had certainly been solved for him very providentially. "I hadn't anything to hide, Mr. Teal. If you'd only let me explain things I could've saved you busting a perfickly good lock and making me miss my boat."

Mr. Teal tilted back his bowler hat with a kind of weary patience.

"Better make it short, Larry," he said. "The night watchman saw you before you coshed him, and he said he'd recognise you again."

"He must've been seeing things," asserted Larry. "Now, if you want to know all about it, Mr. Teal, I saw the doctor the other day, and he told me I was run down. 'What you want, Larry, is a nice holiday,' he says—not that I'd let anyone call me by my first name, you understand, but this doc. is quite a good-class gentleman. 'What you want is a holiday,' he says. 'Why don't you take a sea voyage?' So, seeing I've got an old aunt in Sweden, I thought I'd pay her a visit. Naturally, I thought, the old lady would like to see some newspapers and read how things are going in the old country—"

"And what did she want the stones for?" inquired Teal politely. "Is she making a rock garden?"

"Oh, them?" said Larry innocently. "Them was for my uncle. He's a geo—geo—"

"Geologist is the word you want," said the detective, without smiling. "Now let's go back to

London, and you can write all that down and sign it."

They went back to London with a resigned but still chatty cracksman, though the party lacked some of the high spirits which might have accompanied it. The most puzzled member of it was undoubtedly Larry the Stick, and he spent a good deal of time on the journey trying to think how it could have happened.

He knew that the bonds and jewels had been packed in his suitcase when he left London, for he had gone straight back to his lodgings after he left the Temple Lane Safe Deposit and stowed them away in the bag that was already half filled in anticipation of an early departure. He had dozed in his chair for a few hours, and caught the 7.25 from King's Cross—the bag had never been out of his sight. Except . . . once during the morning he had succumbed to a not unreasonable thirst, and spent half an hour in the restaurant car in earnest collaboration with a bottle of Worthington. But there was no sign of his bag having been tampered with when he came back, and he had seen no familiar face on the train.

It was one of the most mystifying things that had ever happened to him, and the fact that the police case against him had been considerably weakened by his bereavement was a somewhat dubious compensation.

Chief Inspector Teal reached London with a theory of his own. He expounded it to the Assistant Commissioner without enthusiasm.

"I'm afraid there's no doubt that Larry's telling the truth," he said. "He's no more idea what happened to the swag than I have. Nobody

doublecrossed him, because he always works
alone, and he hasn't any enemies that I know of.
There's just one man who might have done it—you
know who I mean."

The Assistant Commissioner sniffed. He had an
irritating and eloquent sniff.

"It would be very tiresome if anything happened
to the Saint," he remarked pointedly. "The C.I.D.
would have a job to find another stock excuse that
would sound quite as convincing."

When Mr. Teal had cooled off in his own room,
he had to admit that there was an element of truth
in the Assistant Commissioner's acidulated comment. It did not mellow his tolerance of the most
unpopular Police Chief of his day; he had had similar thoughts himself, without feeling as if he had
discovered the elixir of life.

The trouble was that the Saint refused to con-
form to any of the traditions which make the capture of the average criminal a mere matter of rou-
tine. There was nothing stereotyped about his
methods which made it easy to include him in the
list of suspects for that particular felony. He was
little more than a name in criminal circles; he had
no jealous associates to give him away, he confided
his plans to no one, he never boasted of his suc-
cesses in anyone's hearing—he did nothing which
gave the police a chance to catch him red-handed.
His name and address were known to every constable in the force; but for all any of them could
prove in a court of law he was an unassailably respectable citizen who had long since left a rather
doubtful past behind him, an amiable young man
about town blessed with plentiful private means,
who had the misfortune to be seen in geographi-

cally close proximity to various lawless events for
which the police could find no suitable scapegoat.
And no one protested their ignorance of everything
to do with him more vigorously than his alleged or
prospective victims. It made things very difficult
for Mr. Teal, who was a clever detective but a
third-rate magician.

The taciturnity of Max Kemmler was a more recent thorn in Mr. Teal's side.

Max Kemmler was a Dane by birth and an
American by naturalisation. The phase of his career in which the United States Federal Authorities
were interested started in St. Louis when he drifted
into Egan's Rats and carved the first notches in his
gun. Prudently, he left St. Louis during an election
clean-up and reappeared in Philadelphia as a
strong-arm man in a news-stand racket. That
lasted him six months, and he left in a hurry; the
tabs caught up with him in New York, where he
went over big for a couple of years as typewriter
expert in an East Side liquor mob. He shot up the
wrong speakie one night after a celebration, and
was lucky to be able to make a passage to
Cherbourg on a French liner that sailed at dawn
the next morning. How he got past the passport
barriers into England was something of a mystery.
He was down on the deportation list, but Scotland
Yard was holding up in the hope of an extradition
warrant.

He was a thick-shouldered man of middle
height, with a taste for camel-hair coats and very
light grey Homburgs. Those who had been able to
keep on the right side of him in the States called
him a good guy—certainly he could put forth a
rugged geniality, when it suited him, which had its

appeal for lesser lights who reckoned it a privilege to be slapped on the back by the notorious Max Kemmler. His cigars were uniformly expensive, and the large diamond set in the corner of his black onyx signet ring conveyed an impression of great substance—he had been paying for it at the rate of two dollars eight-five cents a month until the laborious working-out of the instalment system bored him, and he changed his address.

Max knew from the time he landed that his days in England were numbered, but it was not in his nature to pass up any profitable enterprise on that account. In a very short space of time he had set up a club in a quiet street off the Edgware Road, of which the police had yet to learn. The club boasted a *boule* table, as well as a half-dozen games of *chemin-de-fer,* which were always going: everything was as straight as a die, for Max Kemmler knew that gambling does not need to be crooked to show a long dividend for the bank. The *chemin-de-fer* players paid ten per cent of their winnings to the management, and the smallest chips were priced at half a sovereign. Max did the steering himself and paid his croupiers generously, but he was the only one who made enough out of it to live at the Savoy and put three figures of real money away in his wallet every week in addition.

He had dinner one night with his chief croupier before going north to open the club, and it happened that there was a zealous young detective-sergeant from Vine Street at the next table. It was a small and inexpensive chop-house in Soho, and the detective was not there on business; neither did Max Kemmler know him, for the gambling club was in a different division.

Half-way through the meal Max remembered an enigmatic telephone call that had been put through to his room while he was breakfasting, and asked the croupier about it.

"You ever hear of a guy called Saint?" he queried, and the croupier's jaw fell open.

"Good God!—you haven't heard from *him?*"

Max Kemmler was surprised, to say the least of it.

"Yeah—he did ring me up," he replied guardedly. "What's the matter with you? Is he the wheels in this city?"

The croupier acknowledged, in his own idiom, that Simon Templar was The Wheels. He was a tall, hard-faced man, with iron-grey hair, bushy grey eyebrows and moustache, and the curried complexion of a rather decayed retired major; and he knew much more about the Saint than a law-abiding member of the community should have known. He gave Max Kemmler all the information he wanted, but Max was not greatly impressed.

"What you mean is he's a kind of hijacker, is he? Hard-boiled, huh? I didn't know you'd got any racket like that over here. And he figures *I* ought to pay him for 'protection.' That's funny!" Max Kemmler was grimly amused. "Well, I'd like to see him try it."

"He's tried a lot of things like that and got away with them, Mr. Kemmler," said the croupier awkwardly.

Max turned down one corner of his mouth.

"Yeah? So have I. I guess I'm pretty tough myself, what I mean."

He had a reminder of the conversation the next morning, when a plump and sleepy-looking man called and introduced himself as Chief Inspector Teal.

"I hear you've had a warning from the Saint, Kemmler—one of our men heard you talking about it last night."

Max had done some thinking overnight. He was not expecting to be interviewed by Mr. Teal, but he had his own ideas on the subject that the detective raised.

"What of it?"

"We want to get the Saint, Kemmler. You might be able to help us. Why not tell me some more about it?"

Max Kemmler grinned.

"Sure. Then you know just why the Saint's interested in me, and I can take the rap with him. That dick at the next table ought to have listened some more—then he could have told you I was warned about that one. No thanks, Teal! The Saint and me are buddies together, and he rang me up to ask me to a party. I'm not saying he mightn't get fresh some time, but I can look after that. He might kind of meet with an accident."

It was not the first time that Teal had been met with a similar lack of enthusiasm, and he knew the meaning of the word "no" when it was pushed up to him in a certain way. He departed heavily; and Simon Templar, who was sipping a cocktail within view of the vestibule, watched him go.

"You might think Claud Eustace really wanted to arrest me," he remarked, as the detective's broad back passed through the doors.

His companion, a young man with the air of a gentlemanly prize-fighter, smiled sympathetically. His position was privileged, for it was not many weeks since the Saint's cheerful disregard for the ordinances of the law had lifted him out of a singularly embarrassing situation with a slickness that savoured of sorcery. After all, when you have been youthfully and foolishly guilty of embezzling a large sum of money from your employers in order to try and recoup the losses of an equally youthful and foolish speculation, and a cheque for the missing amount is slipped into your hands by a perfect stranger, you are naturally inclined to see that stranger's indiscretions in an unusual light.

"I wish I had your life," said the young man—his name was Peter Quentin, and he was still very young.

"Brother," said the Saint good-humouredly, "if you had my life you'd have to have my death, which will probably be a sticky one without wreaths. Max Kemmler is a tough egg all right, and you never know."

Peter Quentin stretched out his legs with a wry grimace.

"I don't know that it isn't worth it. Here am I, an A1 proposition to any insurance company, simply wasting everything I've got with no prospect of ever doing anything else. You saved me from getting pushed in clink, but of course there was no hope of my keeping my job. They were very nice and friendly when I confessed and paid in your cheque, but they gave me the air all the same. You can't help seeing their point of view. Once I'd done a thing like that I was a risk to the Company, and next time they mightn't have been so lucky. The result is that I'm one of the great unemployed, and no dole either. If I ever manage to get another job, I shall have to consider myself well off if I'm allowed to sit at an office desk for two hundred and seventy days out of the year, while I get fat and pasty and dream about the pension that'll be no use to me when I'm sixty."

"Instead of which, you want to go on a bread-and-water diet for a ten years' sentence," said the Saint. "I'm a bad example to you, Peter. You ought to meet a girl who'll put all that out of your head."

He really meant what he said. If he refused even to consider his own advice, it was because the perilous charms of the life that he had long ago chosen for his own had woven a spell about him that nothing could break. They were his meat and drink, the wine that made unromantic days worth living, his salute to buccaneers who had had better worlds to conquer. He knew no other life.

Max Kemmler was less poetic about it. He was in the game for what he could get, and he wanted to get it quickly. Teal's visit to him that morning had brought home to him another danger that that accidentally eavesdropping plain-clothes man in the restaurant had thrown across his path. Whatever else the police knew or did not know, they now had the soundest possible reason to believe that Max Kemmler's holiday in England had turned towards profitable business; for nothing else could provide a satisfactory reason for the Saint's interest. His croupier had warned him of that, and Max was taking the warning to heart. The pickings had been good while they lasted, but the time had come for him to be moving.

There was a big play at the club that night. Max Kemmler inspired it, putting forth all the bonhomie that he could call upon to encourage his patrons to lose their shirts and like it. He ordered in half a gross of champagne, and invited the guests to help themselves. He had never worked so hard in his life before, but he saw the results of it when the club closed down at four in the morning and the weary staff counted over the takings. The *boule* table had had a skinner, and money had changed hands so fast in the *chemin-de-fer* parties that the management's ten per cent commission had broken all previous records. Max Kemmler found himself with a comfortingly large wad of crumpled notes to put away. He slapped his croupiers boisterously on the back and opened the last bottle of champagne for them.

"Same time again to-morrow, boys," he said, when he took his leave. "If there's any more jack to come out of this racket, we'll have it."

As a matter of fact, he had no intention of reappearing on the morrow, or on any subsequent day. The croupeirs were due to collect their week's salary the following evening, but that consideration did not influence him. His holiday venture had been even more remunerative than he had hoped, and he was going while the going was good.

Back at the Savoy, he added the wad of notes from his pocket to an even larger wad which came from a sealed envelope which he kept in the hotel manager's safe, and slept with his booty under his pillow.

During his stay in London he had made the acquaintance of a passport specialist. His passage was booked back to Montreal on the *Empress of Britain*, which sailed the next afternoon, and a brand-new Canadian passport established his identity as Max Harford, grain dealer, of Calgary.

He was finishing a sketchy breakfast in his dressing-gown the next morning, when his chief croupier called. Kemmler had a mind to send back a message that he was out, but thought better of it. The croupier would never have come to his hotel unless there was something urgent to tell him, and Max recalled what he had been told about the Saint with a twinge of vague uneasiness.

"What's the trouble, major?" he asked curtly, when the man was shown in.

The other glanced around at the display of strapped and bulging luggage.

"Are you going away, Mr. Kemmler?"

"Just changing my address, that's all," said Kemmler bluffly. "This place is a little too near the high spots—there's always half a dozen bulls snooping around looking for con-men, and I don't like it. It ain't healthy. I'm moving over to a quiet little joint in Bloomsbury, where I don't have to see so many policemen."

"I think you're wise." The croupier sat on the bed and brushed at his hat nervously. "Mr. Kemmler—I thought I ought to come and see you at once. Something has happened."

Kemmler looked at his watch.

"Something's always happening in this busy world," he said with a hearty obtuseness which did not quite carry conviction. "Let's hear about it."

"Well, Mr. Kemmler—I don't quite know how to tell you. It was after we closed down this morning—I was on my way home—"

He broke off with a start as the telephone bell jangled insistently through the room. Kemmler grinned at him emptily, and picked up the receiver.

"Is that you, Kemmler?" said a somnolent voice,

in which a thin thread of excitement was perceptible. "Listen—I'm going to give you a shock, but whatever I say you must not give the slightest indication of what I'm talking about. Don't jump, and don't say anything except 'Yes' or 'No.' "

"Yeah?"

"This is Chief Inspector Teal speaking. Have you got a man with you now?"

"Uh-huh."

"I thought so. That's Simon Templar—the Saint. I just saw him go into the hotel. Never mind if you think you know him. That's his favourite trick. We heard he was planning to hold you up, and we want to get him red-handed. Now what about that idea I mentioned yesterday?"

Kemmler looked round inconspicuously. It was difficult to keep the incredulity out of his eyes. The appearance of his most trusted croupier failed to correspond with the description he had heard of the Saint in any respect except that of height and build. Then he saw that the Anglo-Indian complexion could be a simple concoction of grease paint, the hardness of the features a matter of expression, the greyness of the hair and the bushiness of moustache and eyebrows an elementary problem in make-up.

The croupier was strolling round the bed, and Kemmler could scarcely control himself as he saw the man touch the pillow underneath which the envelope of notes still lay.

"Well?"

Kemmler fought out a battle with himself of which nothing showed on his face. The Saint's right hand was resting in a side pocket of his coat —there was nothing in that ordinary fact to disturb most people, but to Max Kemmler it had a particular and deadly significance. And his own gun was under the pillow with the money—he had been hoodwinked like the veriest greenhorn.

"What about it?" he demanded as calmly as he could.

"We want to get him," said the detective. "If he's in your room already you can't do a thing. Why not be sensible? You're sailing on the *Empress of Britain* to-day, and that suits us. We'll turn a blind eye on your new passport. We won't even ask why the Saint wants to rob you. All we ask is for you to help us get that man."

Max Kemmler swallowed. That knowledge of his secret plans was only the second blow that had come to him. He was a tough guy in any circumstances, but he knew when the dice were loaded against him. He was in a cleft stick. The fact that he had promised himself the pleasure of giving the Saint an unwholesome surprise if they ever met didn't enter into it.

"What shall I do?" he asked.

"Let him get on with it. Let him stick you up. Don't fight or anything. I'll have a squad of men outside your door in thirty seconds."

"Okay," said Max Kemmler expressionlessly. "I'll see to it."

He put down the receiver and looked into the muzzle of Simon Templar's automatic. With the detective's warning still ringing in his ears, he let his mouth fall open in well-simulated astonishment and wrath.

"What the hell—"

"Spare my virginal ears," said the Saint gently. "It's been swell helping you to rake in the berries,

Max, but this is where the game ends. Stick your hands right up and feel your chest expand!''

He turned over the pillow and put Kemmler's gun in a spare pocket. The envelope of notes went into another. Max Kemmler watched the disappearance of his wealth with a livid face of fury that he could hardly control. If he had not received that telephone call he would have leapt at the Saint and chanced it.

Simon smiled at him benevolently.

"I'm afraid we'll have to see that you don't raise an alarm," he said. "Would you mind turning round?"

Max Kemmler turned round reluctantly. He was not prepared for the next thing that happened to him, and it is doubtful whether even Chief Inspector Teal could have induced him to submit meekly to it if he had. Fortunately he was given no option. A reversed gun-butt struck him vimfully and scientifically on the occiput, and he collapsed in a limp heap.

When he woke up a page-boy was shaking him by the shoulder and his head with splitting with the worst headache that he had ever experienced.

"Is your luggage ready to go, Mr. Kemmler?"

Kemmler glared at the boy for a few seconds in silence. Then recollection returned to him, and he staggered up with a hoarse profanity.

He dashed to the door and flung it open. The corridor was deserted.

"Where's that guy who was here a minute ago? Where are the dicks?" he shouted, and the bell-hop gaped at him uncomprehendingly.

"I don't know, sir."

Max Kemmler flung him aside and grabbed at

the telephone. In a few seconds he was through to Scotland Yard—and Chief Inspector Teal.

"Say, you, what the hell's the idea? What is it, huh? The grand double-cross? Where are those dicks who were going to be waiting for the Saint outside my door? What've you done with 'em? You big paluka—"

"I don't understand you, Kemmler," said Mr. Teal coldly. "Will you tell me exactly what's happened?"

"The Saint's been here. You know it. You rang me up and told me. You told me to *let* him stick me up—*give* him everything he wanted—you wouldn't let me put up a fight—you said you'd be waiting for him outside the door and catch him red-handed—"

Kemmler babbled on for a while longer; and then gradually his tale petered out incoherently as he realised just how easily he had been hoodwinked.

When the detective came to interview him Kemmler apologised and said he must have been drunk, which nobody believed.

But it seemed as if the police didn't know anything about his passage on the *Empress of Britain* after all. It was Max Kemmler's only consolation.

THE BAD BARON

"In these days of strenuous competiton," said the Saint, "it's an extraordinarily comforting thing to know you're at the top of your profession—unchallenged, undismayed, and wholly beautiful."

His audience listened to him with a very fair simulation of reverence—Patricia Holm because she had heard similar modest statements so often before that she was beginning to believe them, Peter Quentin because he was the very latest recruit to the cause of Saintly lawlessness and the game was still new and exciting.

For the Saint certainly had a rival; and of recent days a combination of that rival's boundless energy and Simon Templar's cautious self-effacement had placed another name in the position in the headlines which had once been regularly booked for the Saint. Newspapers screamed his exploits from their bills; music-hall comedians gagged about him; detectives tore their hair and endured the scathing criticisms of the Press and their superiors with as much fortitude as they could call on; and owners of valuable jewellery hurriedly deposited their valuables in safes and found a new interest in patent burglar alarms.

For jewels were the specialty of the man who was known as "The Fox"—there was very little else known about him. He burst upon the public in a racket of sensational banner lines when he held up Lady Palfrey's charity ball at Grosvenor House single-handed, and got clear away with nearly ten thousand pounds worth of display pieces. The clamour aroused by that exploit had scarcely passed its peak when he raided Sir Barnaby Gerrald's house in Berkeley Square and took a four-thousand-pound pearl necklace from a wall safe in the library while the Gerralds were entertaining a distinguished company to dinner in the next room. He opened and ransacked a Bond Street jeweller's strong-room the very next night at a cost to the insurance underwriters of over twelve thousand pounds. Within a week he was the topic of every conversation: Geneva Conferences were relegated to obscure corners of the news sheets, and even Wimbledon took second place.

All three coups showed traces of careful preliminary spade-work. It was obvious that the Fox had mapped out every move in advance, and that the headlines were merely proclaiming the results of a scheme of operations that had been maturing perhaps for years. It was equally obvious to surmise that the crimes which had already been committed were not the beginning and the end of the campaign. News editors (who rarely possess valuable jewels) seized on the Fox as a Heaven-sent gift in a flat season; and the Fox worked for them with a sense of news value that was something like the answer to their blasphemous prayers. He entered Mrs. Wilbur G. Tully's suite at the Dorchester and removed her jewel-case with everything that it contained while she was in the bathroom and her maid had been decoyed away on a false errand. Mrs. Tully sobbingly told the reporters that there was only one thing which could never be replaced—a diamond-and-amethyst pendant valued at a mere two hundred pounds, a legacy from her mother, for which she was prepared to offer a reward of twice its value. It was returned to her through the post the next morning, with a typewritten expression of the Fox's sincere apologies. The news editors bought cigars and wallowed in their Hour. They hadn't had anything as good as that since the Saint appeared to go out of business, and they made the most of it.

It was even suggested that the Fox might be the once notorious Saint in a new guise; and Simon Templar received a visit from Chief Inspector Teal.

"For once I'm not guilty, Claud," said the Saint, with considerable sadness; and the detective knew him well enough to believe him.

Simon had his private opinions about the Fox. The incident of Mrs. Tully's ancestral pendant did not appeal to him; he bore no actual ill-will towards Mrs. Tully, but the very prompt return of the article struck him as being a very ostentatious gesture to the gallery of a kind in which he had never indulged. Perhaps he was prejudiced. There is very little room for friendly rivalry in the paths of crime; and the Saint had his own human egotisms.

The fame of the Fox was brought home to him that evening through another line.

"There's a man who's asking for trouble," said Peter Quentin.

He pointed to a copy of the *Evening News* as it lay open on the table between the glasses. Simon leaned sideways and scanned it lazily.

THE MAN WHO IS NOT AFRAID OF BURGLARS

Three times attacked—

three times the winner
NO QUARTER!

BARON VON DORTVENN is one visitor to London who is not likely to spend any sleepless nights on account of the wave of crime with which the police are trying in vain to cope.

He has come to England to look after the bracelet of Charlemagne, which he is lending to the International Jewellery Exhibition which opens on Monday.

The famous bracelet is a massive circle of gold four inches wide and thickly encrusted with rubies. It weighs eight pounds, and is virtually priceless.

At present it is locked in the drawer of an ordinary desk at the house in Campden Hill which the Baron has rented for a short season. He takes it with him wherever he goes. It has been in the care of his family for five centuries, and the Baron regards it as a mascot.

Baron von Dortvenn scorns the precautions which would be taken by most people who found themselves in charge of such a priceless heirloom.

"Every criminal is a coward," the Baron

told an *Evening News* representative yesterday. "I have been attacked three times in the
course of my travels with the bracelet—"

"Sounds like a job for our friend the Fox," remarked Peter Quentin carelessly; and was amazed
at the look Simon Templar gave him. It leapt from
the Saint's eyes like blued steel.

"Think so?" drawled the Saint.

He skimmed down the rest of the half-column,
which was mainly concerned with the Baron's
boasts of what he would do to anyone who attempted to steal his heirloom. Half-way down
there was an inset photograph of a typical Junker
with a double chin, close-cropped hair, monocle,
and waxed moustaches. Underneath it there was a
cut line saying "Baron von Dortvenn," in case any
reader should mistake it for a portrait of Mr. Jack
Buchanan's new leading lady.

"A nasty-looking piece of work," said the Saint
thoughtfully.

Patricia Holm finished her Bronx rather quickly.
She knew all the signs—and only that afternoon
the Saint had hinted that he might behave himself
for a week.

"I'm starving," she said.

They went down to the grill-room, and the subject might have been forgotten during the Saint's
profound study of the menu and wine list, for Simon had a very delicate discrimination in the lux-
uries of life. Let us say that the subject *might* have
been forgotten—the opportunity to forget it simply
did not arise.

"To get the best out of caviar, you should eat it
like they do in Rumania—in half-pound portions,
with a soup-ladle," said the Saint, when the cloud

of bustling waiters had dispersed.

And then he relaxed in his chair. Relaxed completely, and lighted a cigarette with infinite deliberation.

"Don't look round," he said. "The gent has got to pass our table. Just put it on the record that I only said I was blowed."

The other two gazed at him vaguely and waited. A superb *chef de restaurant* came past, ushering a mixed pair of guests to a table on the other side of the room. One of them was a blonde girl, smartly dressed and rather good-looking in a statuesque way. The other was unmistakably the Baron von Dortvenn.

Simon could hardly keep his eyes off them. He barely trifled with his food, sipped his wine with no more interest than if it had been water, and lighted one cigarette from another with monotonous regularity. When the orchestra changed over to a dance rhythm, he pleaded that he was suffering from corns and left it to Peter Quentin to take Patricia on the floor.

The Baron was apparently not so afflicted. He danced several times with his companion, and danced very badly. It was after a particularly elephantine waltz that Simon saw the girl, quite openly, dab her eyes with her handkerchief as she left the floor.

He leaned back even more lazily, with his eyes half closed and a cigarette merely smouldering in the corner of his mouth, and continued to watch. The couple were admirably placed for his observations—the girl was facing him, and he saw the Baron in profile. And it became very plain to him that a jolly *soirée* was definitely not being had by all.

The girl and the Baron were arguing—not loudly but very vehemently—and the Baron was getting red in the face. He was clearly working himself into a vicious rage, and wrath did not make him look any more savoury. The girl was trying to be dignified, but she was breaking down. Suddenly, with a flash of spirit, she said something that obviously struck home. The Baron's eyes contracted, and his big hand fastened on the girl's wrists. Simon could see the knuckles whitening under the skin in the savage brutality of the grip, and the girl winced. The Baron released her with a callous fling of his arm that spilled a fork off the table; and without another word the girl gathered up her wrap and walked away.

She came towards the Saint on her way to the door. He saw that her eyes were faintly rimmed with red, but he liked the steady set of her mouth. Her steps were a little uncertain; as she reached his table she swayed and brushed against it, slopping over a few drops from a newly-filled wineglass.

"I'm awfully sorry," she said in a low voice.

The Saint snapped a match between his fingers, and held her eyes.

"I saw what happened—let me get you a taxi."

He stood up and came round the table while she started to protest. He led her up the stairs and through the lobby to the street.

"Really—it's awfully nice of you to bother—"

"To tell you the truth," murmured the Saint, "I have met people with a better taste in barons."

The commissionaire hailed a taxi at the Saint's

nod, and the girl gave an address in St. John's Wood. Simon allowed her to thank him again, and coolly followed her in before the commissionaire closed the door. The taxi pulled out from the kerb before she could speak.

"Don't worry," said the Saint. "I was just feeling like a breath of fresh air, and my intentions are fairly honourable. I should probably have been obliged to smite your Baron on the nose if you hadn't left him when you did. Here—have a cigarette. It'll make you feel better."

The girl took the smoke from his case. They were held up a few yards further on, at the end of Piccadilly; and suddenly the door of the taxi was flung open and a breathless man in a doublebreasted dinner jacket appeared in the aperture.

"Pardon madame—I did not sink I should catch you. It is yours, isn't it?"

He held up a small drop ear-ring; and as he turned his head Simon recognised him as a solitary diner from a table adjoining his own.

"Oh!" The girl sat up, biting her lip. "Thank you —thank you so much—"

"*Il n'y a pas de quoi, madame,*" said the man happily. "I see it fall and I run after you, but always you're too quick. Now it's all right. I am content. Madame, you permit me to say you are a brave woman? I also saw everysing. Zat Baron—"

All at once the girl hid her face in her hands.

"I don't know how to thank you," she said chokingly. "You're all so sweet . . . Oh, my God! If only I could kill him! He deserves to be killed. He deserves to lose his beastly bracelet. I'd steal it myself—"

"Ah, but then you would be in prison, madame—"

"Oh, it'd be easy enough. It's on tne ground floor—you'd only have to break open the desk. He doesn't believe in burglar-alarms. He's so sure of himself. But I'd show him. I'd make him pay!"

She turned away to the corner and sobbed hysterically.

Simon glanced at the little Frenchman.

"*Elle se trouvera mieux chez elle,*" he said; and the other nodded sympathetically and closed the door.

The taxi drew away in a wedge of traffic and turned up Regent Street. Simon sat back in his corner and let the girl have her cry. It was the best possible thing for her; and he could have said nothing helpful.

They had a practically clear run through to St. John's Wood; and the girl recovered a little as they neared their destination. She wiped her eyes and took out a microscopic powder-puff, with the unalterable vanity of women.

"You must think I'm a fool," she said, as the taxi slowed up. "Perhaps I am. But no one else can understand."

"I don't mind," said the Saint.

The cab stopped, and he leaned across her to open the door. Her face was within two inches of his, and the Saint required all adventures to be complete. In his philosophy, knight-errantry had its own time-honoured rewards.

His lips touched hers unexpectedly; and then in a flash, with a soft laugh, he was out of the taxi. She walked past him and went up the steps of the house without looking back.

Simon rode back jubilantly to the Piccadilly, and found his lady and Peter Quentin patiently ordering more coffee. The Baron had already left.

"I saw you leaving with the blonde Venus," said Peter enviously. "How on earth did you work it?"

"Is this a new romance?" smiled Patricia.

"You want to be careful of these barons," said Peter. "Next thing you know, you'll have a couple of his pals clicking their heels at you and inviting you to meet him in Hyde Park at dawn."

The Saint calmly annexed Peter Quentin's liqueur and tilted his chair backwards. Over the rim of his glass he exchanged bows with the chivalrous Frenchman at the adjoining table, who was paying off his bill and preparing to leave; and then he surveyed the other two with a lazily reckless glint in his eye that could have only one meaning.

"Let's go home," he said.

They sauntered in silence down Piccadilly to the block where the Saint's flat was situated; and there the Saint doffed his hat with a flourish, and kissed Patricia's hand.

"Lady, be good. Peter and I have a date to watch the moon rising over the Warrington waterworks."

In the same silence two immaculately dressed young men sauntered on to the garage where the Saint kept his car. Nothing was said until one of them was at the wheel, with the other beside him, and the great silver Hirondel was humming smoothly past Hyde Park Corner. Then the fair-haired one spoke.

"Campden Hill," I suppose?"

"You said it," murmured the Saint. "Baron von

Dortvenn has asked for it once too often."

He drove slowly past the house for which Baron von Dortvenn had exchanged the *schloss* that was doubtless his more natural background. It was a gaunt Victorian edifice, standing apart from the adjacent houses in what for London was an unusually large garden, surrounded by a six-foot brick wall topped by iron spikes. As far as the Saint could see, it was in darkness; but he was not really concerned to know whether the Baron had come home or whether he had passed on to seek a more amenable candidate for his favours in one of the few night clubs that the police had not yet closed down. Simon Templar was out for justice, and he could not find his opportunity too soon.

Twenty yards beyond the house he disengaged the gear lever and swung himself out on to the running-board while the car was coasting to a standstill. It was then only half-past eleven, but the road was temporarily deserted.

"Turn the bus round, Peter, and pretend to be tinkering with the engine. Hop back into it at the first sounds of any excitement, and be on your toes for a quick getaway. I know it's bad technique to plunge into a burglary without getting the lie of the land first, but I shall sleep like a child to-night if I have the bracelet of Charlemagne under my mattress."

"You aren't going in alone," said Peter Quentin firmly.

He had the door on his side of the car open; but the Saint caught his shoulder.

"I am, old lad. I'm not making a fully-fledged felon of you sooner than I can help—and if we were both inside there'd be no one to cover the retreat if the Baron's as hot as he tells the world.''

His tone forbade argument. There was a quietly metallic timbre in it that would have told any listener that this was the Saint's own private picnic. And the Saint smiled. He punched Peter Quentin gently in the biceps, and was gone.

The big iron gates that gave entrance to the garden were locked—he discovered that at the first touch. He went on a few yards and hooked his fingers over the top of the wall. One quick, springy heave, and he was on top of the wall, clambering gingerly over the spikes. As he did so he glanced towards the house, and saw a wisp of black shadow detach itself from the neighbourhood of a ground-floor window and flit soundlessly across a strip of lawn into the cover of a clump of laurels.

The Saint dropped inside the garden on his toes, and stood there swiftly knotting a handkerchief over the lower part of his face. The set of his lips was a trifle grim. Someone else was on the job that night—he had only just arrived in time.

He slipped along the side of a hedge towards the spot where the black shadow had disappeared; but he had underrated the first intruder's power of silent movement. There was a sudden scuff of shoes on the turf behind him, and the Saint swerved and ducked like lightning. Something whizzed past his head and struck his shoulder a numbing blow: he shot out an arm and grabbed hold of a coat, jerking his assailant towards him. His left hand felt for the man's throat.

It was all over very quickly, without any noise. Simon lowered the unconscious man to the ground, and flashed the dimmed beam of a tiny pocket torch on his face. A black mask covered it

—Simon whipped it off and saw the sallow face of the Frenchman who had followed him with the unfortunate girl's ear-ring.

The Saint snapped off his flashlight and straightened up with his mouth pursed in a noiseless whistle that widened into a smile. Verily, he was having a night out. . . .

He glided across the lawn to the nearest window, feeling around for the catch with a thin knife-blade. In three seconds it gave way, and he slid up the sash and climbed nimbly over the sill. His feet actually landed on the baronial desk. The top drawer was locked: he squeezed a fine steel claw in above the lock and levered adroitly. The drawer burst open with a crash, and the beam of his torch probed its interior. Almost the first thing he saw was a heavy circlet of dull yellow, which caught the light from a hundred crimson facets studded over its surface. Simon picked it up and shoved it into his pocket. Its great weight dragged his coat all over on one side.

And at that moment all the lights in the room went on.

The Saint whirled round.

He looked into the single black eye of an automatic held in the hand of Baron von Dortvenn himself. On either side of the Baron was a heavily-built, hard-faced man.

"So you're the Fox?" said the Baron genially.

Simon thanked heaven for the handkerchief that covered his face. The two hard-faced men were advancing towards him, and one of them jingled a pair of handcuffs.

"On the contrary," said the Saint, "I'm the Bishop of Bootle and Upper Tooting."

He held out his wrists resignedly. For a moment the man with the handcuffs was between him and the Baron's automatic, and the Saint took his chance. His left whizzed round in a terrific hook that smacked cleanly to its mark on the side of the man's jaw, and Simon leapt on to the desk. He went through the window in a flying dive, somersaulted over his hands, and was on his feet again in an instant.

He sprinted across the lawn and went over the wall like a cat. A whistle screamed into the night behind him, and he saw Peter Quentin tumble into the car as he jumped down to the pavement. Simon stepped on to the running-board as the Hirondel streaked past, and fell over the side into the seat beside the driver.

"Give her the gun," he ordered briefly, "and dodge as you've never dodged before. I think they'll be after us."

"What happened?" asked Peter Quentin; and the Saint unfastened the handkerchief from his face and grinned.

"It looks like they were waiting for someone," he said.

It took twenty minutes of brilliant driving to satisfy the Saint that they were safe from any possible pursuit. On the way Simon took the heavy jewelled armlet from his pocket and gazed at it lovingly under one of the dash-board lamps.

"That's one thing the Fox didn't put over," he said cryptically.

He was breakfasting off bacon and eggs the next morning at eleven o'clock when Peter Quentin walked in. Peter carried a morning paper, which he tossed into the Saint's lap.

"There's something for your 'Oh, yeah?' album," he said grimly.

Simon poured out a cup of coffee.

"What is it—some more intelligent utterances by Cabinet Ministers?"

"You'd better read it," said Peter. "It looks as if several people made mistakes last night."

Simon Templar picked up the paper and stared at the double-column splash.

"THE FOX" CAPTURED
C.I.D. Wakes Up
BRILLIANT COUP IN KENSINGTON

ONE OF THE CLEVEREST STRATAGEMS in the history of Criminal Detection achieved its object at eleven-thirty last night with the arrest of Jean-Baptiste Arvaille, alleged to be the famous jewel thief known as "The Fox."

Arvaille will be charged at the police court this morning with a series of audacious robberies totalling over fifty thousand pounds.

It will be told how Inspector Henderson, of Scotland Yard, assisted by a woman member of the Special Branch, posed as "Baron von Dortvenn" and baited the trap with a mythical "bracelet of Charlemagne" which he was stated to have brought to England for the International Jewellery Exhibition.

The plot owes much of its success to the co-operation of the Press, which gave the fullest possible publicity to the "Baron's" arrival.

It was stated in this newspaper yesterday that the "bracelet of Charlemagne" was a circle of solid gold thickly encrusted with rubies.

In actual fact it is made of lead, thinly plated with gold, and the stones in it are worthless imitations. Workmen sworn to secrecy created it specially for Inspector Henderson's use.

Simon Templar read through the whole detailed story. After which he was speechless for some time.

And then he smiled.

"Oh, well," he said, "it isn't everyone who can say he's kissed a woman policeman."

THE BRASS BUDDHA

"Have another drink," said Sir Ambrose
Grange.

He was a man with a lot to say, but that was his
theme song. He had used it so many times during
the course of that evening that Simon Templar had
begun to wonder whether Sir Ambrose imagined
he had invented a new and extraordinarily subtle
philosophy, and was patiently plugging it at intervals until his audience grasped the point. It
bobbed up along the line of his conversation like
vitamins in a food reformer's menu. Tapping re-
sources which seemed equally inexhaustible, he
delved into the kit-bag of memory for reminis-
cences and into his trouser pockets for the price of
beer; and the Saint obliged him by absorbing both
with equal courtesy.

"Yes, sir," resumed Sir Ambrose, when their
glasses had been refilled. "Business is business.
That is my motto, and it always will be. If you happen to know that something is valuable, and the
other fellow doesn't, you have every right to buy it

61

from him at his price without disclosing your knowledge. He gets what he thinks is a fair price, you get your profit, and you're both satisfied. Isn't that what goes on every day on the Stock Exchange? If you receive inside information that certain shares are going to rise, you buy as many as you can. You probably never meet the man who sells them to you, but that doesn't alter the fact of what you're doing. You're deliberately taking advantage of your knowledge to purchase something for a fraction of its value, and it never occurs to you that you ought to tell the seller that if he held on to his shares for another week he could make all the profit for himself."

"Quite," murmured the Saint politely.

"And so," said Sir Ambrose, patting the Saint's knee impressively with his flabby hand, "when I heard that the path of the new by-pass road cut straight through the middle of that old widow's property, what did I do? Did I go to her and say, 'Madam, in another week or two you'll be able to put your own price on this house, and any bank or building society would be glad to lend you enough to pay off this instalment of the mortgage'? Why, if I'd done anything like that I should have been a fool, sir—a sentimental old fool. Of course I didn't. It was the old geeser's own fault if she was too stupid and doddering to know what was going on around her. I simply foreclosed at once; and in three weeks I'd sold her house for fifteen times as much as I gave her for it. That's business." Sir Ambrose chortled wheezily over the recollection. "By Gad, you should have seen the old trout's face when she heard about it. And was she rude? By Gad, if words could break bones I should be wheeling myself about in an invalid chair still. But that kind of thing doesn't worry *me* . . . Have another drink."

"Have one with me," suggested the Saint half-heartedly; but Sir Ambrose waved the invitation aside.

"No, sir. I never allow a young man to pay for my drinks. Have a good time with me. The same again?"

Simon nodded, and lighted a cigarette while Sir Ambrose toddled over to the bar. He was a pompous and rather tubby little man, with a waxed moustache that matched his silver-grey spats, and a well-wined complexion that matched the carnation in his buttonhole; and the Saint did not like him. In fact, running over a lengthy list of gentlemen of whom he had gravely disapproved, Simon Templar found it difficult to name anyone whom he had felt less inclined to take into his bosom with vows of eternal brotherhood.

He disliked Sir Ambrose no less heartily because he had known him less than a couple of hours. With an idle evening to spend by himself, the Saint had sailed out into the West End to pass it as entertainingly as he could. He had no plans whatever, but his faith in the beneficence of the gods was sublime. Thus he had gone in search of adventure before, and he had rarely been disappointed. To him, the teeming thousands of assorted souls who jostled through the sky-sign area on a Saturday night were so many oysters who might be opened by a man with the clairvoyant eye and delicate touch which the Saint claimed for his genius. It was a business of drifting where the whim guided him, following an impulse and hoping that it might lead to an interest, taking a chance and not caring if it failed.

In just that spirit of careless optimism he had wandered into a small hotel in a quiet street behind the Strand and discovered an almost deserted bar where he could imbibe a glass of ale while seeking inspiration for his next move. And it was there that a casual remark about the weather had floated him into the acquaintance of Sir Ambrose Grange. It was only a matter of minutes after that before Sir Ambrose, having presented his card, pulled out the opening chord of his theme song and said: "Have a drink?"

Simon had a drink. Even before the state of the weather arose as an introduction, he had felt a professional curiosity to know whether anybody could be quite as unsavoury a bore as Sir Ambrose looked. And he had not been disappointed. Within five minutes Sir Ambrose had him sitting in a corner listening to the details of an ingenious trick he had invented as a boy at school of swindling his contemporaries out of their weekly ration of toffee. Within ten minutes Sir Ambrose was leading on to a description of the smart deals on a larger scale which had built up his comfortable fortune. He seemed to have had several drinks on his own before he started intoning his chorus to the Saint. The effects of them had been to make him loquacious and confidential, but they had not added to his charm. And the more cordially Simon learned to detest him, the more intently Simon listened—for it had dawned on the Saint that perhaps this evening was being well spent.

Sir Ambrose returned with steps that could have

been steadier, and slopped over some of the beer as he deposited their glasses on the table. He sat down again and leaned back with a sigh of large-waisted well-being.

"Yes, sir," he resumed tirelessly. "Sentiment is no good. My uncle was sentimental, and what did it do for him?"

Not having known Sir Ambrose's uncle, Simon found the question unanswerable.

"It made him a pest to his heirs," said Sir Ambrose, solving the riddle. "That's what it did. Not that he left much for us to inherit—a beggarly ten thousand odd was all that he managed to keep out of the hands of the parasites who traded on his soft heart. But what did he do with it?"

Once again the Saint was nonplussed. Sir Ambrose, however, did not really require assistance.

"Look at this," he said.

He dragged a small brass image out of his pocket and set it up on the table between the glasses. Simon glanced at it, and recognised it at once. It was one of those pyramidal figures of a seated Buddha, miniatures of the gigantic statue at Kamakura, which find their place in every tourists' curio shop from Karachi to Yokohama.

"That, sir," said the sentimentalist's nephew, "was my uncle's. He bought it in Shanghai when he was a young man, and he called it his mascot. He used to burn a joss-stick in front of it every day—said the ju-ju wouldn't work without it. And then, when he died, what do you think we found in his will?"

Simon was getting accustomed to Sir Ambrose's

interrogative style, but the Saint was not very easily silenced.

"A thousand quid to buy joss-sticks," he hazarded.

Sir Ambrose shook his head rather impatiently, till both his chins wobbled.

"No, sir. Something much worse than that. We found that not a penny of his money could be touched until this ridiculous thing had been sold for two thousand pounds. He said that only a man who was prepared to pay a sum like that for it would appreciate it properly and give it the attention he wanted. Personally, I think that anyone who paid a sum like for it could be put in a lunatic asylum without a certificate. But there it is in the will, and the lawyers say we can't upset it. I've been carrying the damned thing about with me half the week, showing it to all the antique shops in London, and the best offer I've had is fifteen shillings."

"But surely," said the Saint, "you could get a friend of yours to buy it, and give him the two thousand back with a spot of interest as soon as the executors unbuttoned?"

"If anything like that could have been done, sir, I'd have done it. But the old fool thought of that himself, and he left strict instructions that the executors were to be satisfied beyond all possible doubt that the sale was a genuine one. And he made his bank the executors, damn him! If you've ever tried to put anything over on a bank you'll know what a hope we've got of doing anything like that. No—the best thing we can ever hope to do is to find some genuine stranger and sell it to him while he's drunk."

Simon picked up the image and examined it closely. It was unexpectedly heavy, and he guessed that the brass casting must have been filled with lead. On the base there was a line of Chinese characters cut into the metal and filled with red.

"Funny language," observed Sir Ambrose, leaning over to point to the characters. "I've often wanted to meet a Chinese who could tell me what they write on things like this. Look at that thing there like a tadpole with wings. I'll bet that's a particularly dirty swear—it's twice the size of the other words. Have a drink."

The Saint looked at his watch.

"I'm afraid I'll have to be getting home," he observed.

"Come and see me one evening," said Sir Ambrose. "You've got my address on my card, and I like young company. Come along one night next week, and I'll invite some girls."

Simon reached his flat in time to see Peter Quentin and Patricia Holm climbing out of a taxi. They were in evening dress, and the Saint surveyed them rudely.

"Well," he said, "have you mugs finished pretending to be numbers one and two of the Upper Ten?"

"He's jealous," said Patricia, on Peter Quentin's arm. "His own tails have been in pawn so long that the moth's done them in."

A misguided friend had presented the Saint with tickets for the Opera. Simon Templar, in one of his fits of perversity, had stated in no uncertain terms that it was too hot to put on a starched shirt and listen to perspiring tenors dying in C flat for four hours, and Peter Quentin had volunteered to be Patricia's escort.

"We thought of some bacon and eggs," Peter said, "and wondered if you'd like to treat us."

"I thought you might treat me," murmured the Saint. "As an inducement for me to be seen out with a girl whose clothes have all slipped down below her waist, and a pie-faced tough disguised as a waiter, it's the least you can offer."

Back in the taxi, they asked him how he had spent his evening.

"I've been drinking beer with one of the most septic specimens in London," said the Saint thoughtfully. "And if I can't make him wish he hadn't told me so much about himself I won't have another bath for six years."

The problem of securing an adequate contribution towards his old age pension from Sir Ambrose Grange occupied the Saint's mind considerably for the next twenty-four hours. Sir Ambrose had gratuitously introduced himself as such a perfect example of the type of man whom the Saint prayed to meet that Simon felt that his reputation was at stake. Unless something suitably unpleasant happened to Sir Ambrose in a very short space of time, the Saint would sink down to somewhere near zero in his own estimation of himself—a possibility that was altogether too dreadful to contemplate.

He devoted most of the Sabbath to revolving various schemes in his mind, all of which were far less holy than the day; but he had not finally decided on any of them when the solution literally fell into his arms by a coincidence that seemed too good to be true.

This happened on the Monday afternoon.

He sallied out of his flat into Piccadilly in the hope of finding a paper with the winner of the Eclipse Stakes, and as he stepped on to the pavement a middle-aged man in horn-rimmed spectacles and a Panama who was hurrying past suddenly staggered in his direction, and would have fallen if the Saint had not caught him. Several passers-by turned and watched curiously; and Simon Templar, whose ideas of grandstanding heroism were not of that type, was tempted to deposit the middle-aged gent tenderly on the sidewalk and let him do his dying gladiator act alone. The man in the Panama was no human hairpin, and his legs seemed to have turned to rubber.

Then Simon saw that the man's eyes were open. He grinned at the Saint crookedly.

"Sorry, stranger," he said, in the broadest Yankee. "I'll be okay in a minute. Been trying to do too much after my operation, I guess—the doc told me I'd crack up if I didn't take it easy. . . . Gosh, look at the rubbernecks waitin' to see me die! Say, do you live in there? Is there a foyer I can sit down in? I don't wanna be stared at like I was the Nelson Monument."

Simon helped the man inside and sat him on a settee beside the lift. The Yank tipped off his Panama and wiped his forehead with a bandanna handkerchief.

"Just four days outa the hospital, and tearin' about like a fool for two of 'em. And missed my lunch to-day. That's what's done it. Say, is there a public telephone here? I promised to meet my wife an hour ago, and she must think I made myself a street accident."

"I'm afraid there isn't," said the Saint. "This is just a block of flats."

"Well, I guess I'll just be bawled out. Gosh, but that poor kid'll be worried stiff."

Simon looked up at the clock. He was in no great hurry.

"You can phone from my flat if you like," he said. "It's on the first floor."

"Say, that's real white of you!"

The Saint helped him into the elevator, and they shot upwards. Settled in an armchair beside the telephone, the American made a reassuring call to the Savoy Hotel number. Simon thought it was excessively sloppy, but it was not his business.

"Well, that's that," said his guest, when the gush was over. "I guess I owe you something for your kindness. Have a cigar?"

Simon accepted a weed. It was a large fat one, with a lovely picture on the band.

"Think of me cracking up like that in your arms!" prattled the American, whose vocal cords at least seemed unimpaired. "Gosh, you musta thought I was something out of a flowerbed. I didn't know they could take that much outa you along with your appendix. And all this fuss just to find a damn brass Buddha! Gosh, it makes you wonder what nut started this collecting game."

The Saint, with a match half-way to his cigar, stared at him till the flame scorched his fingers.

"Brass Buddha?" he said faintly. "Who wants a brass Buddha?"

"Louis Froussard wants one, if that means anything to you, stranger. Say, but here I am in your apartment, and you don't even know my name. Allow me." The American dug out his wallet, extracted a card, and handed it over. "James G. Amberson, at your service. Any time you want one of Napoleon's skulls, or the original pajamas the Queen of Sheba gave to King Solomon—I'm the man to go and find 'em. Yes, sir. That's my job—huntin' for missing links for museums and millionaires who feel they gotta collect something so's they can give the reporters something to write about. That's me."

"And you want a brass Buddha?" said the Saint almost caressingly.

James G. Amberson (according to his card, the G. stood for Gardiner, which the Saint thought was very modest—it might have been Gabriel) flapped a raw-boned hand deprecatingly.

"Aw, you ain't gonna offer me the thing your auntie brought home last time she went on a world cruise, are you?" he pleaded. "That's what I been getting every place I've tried. Everyone in London's got a brass Buddha, but none of 'em is the right one. This one's a special one—you wouldn't know it to look at it, but it is. Some Chinese emperor back in about two million B.C. had three of 'em made for his three daughters, who were no better than they shoulda been, accordin' to history—you don't wanna know all that hooey, do you? I guess I'm a bit fuddled over it myself. But, anyhow, Lou Froussard has got two of 'em, and he wants the third. I gotta find it. Sounds like I'd taken on a long job, don't it?"

Simon drew on his cigar a little less impetuously.

"How will you know this particular one when you find it?" he asked.

"Say, that's easy. It's gotta little Chinese dedication carved in the base and filled with red paint. I don't know any language expect plain English, but this daughter's name comes in the dedication, and I got a Chinese to show me what it looked like —Gosh, is that cigar corked or something?"

"No—it's a swell cigar. Would you mind showing me what this name looks like?"

The American's eyes opened rather blankly, but he took out a pencil and sketched a character on the back of an envelope.

"There she is, stranger. Say, you're looking at me like I was a mummy come to life. What's the matter?"

The Saint filled his lungs. For him, the day had suddenly bloomed out into a rich surpassing beauty that only those who have shared his delight in damaging the careers of pompous old sinners with bushy grey face-hair can understand. The radiance of his own inspiration dazzled him.

"Nothing's the matter," he said seraphically. "Nothing on earth could be the matter on a day like this. How many millions will your Mr. Froussard give for that Buddha?"

"Well, millions is a large word," said Amberson cautiously, looking at the Saint in not unreasonable perplexity. "But I guess I could pay fifteen thousand iron men for it."

"You find the iron men, and I'll find your Buddha," said the Saint.

The American grinned, and stood up.

"I don't know whether you've got an ace in the hole or whether you're just pulling my leg," he remarked; "but if you can find that Buddha the fifteen grand are waitin' for you. Say, but I'm real grateful to you for helpin' me out like this. Come to the Savoy and have lunch to-morrow—and you can bring the Buddha with you if you've found it."

"Thanks," said the Saint. "I'll do both."

He showed Amberson to the door, and came straight back to grab the telephone. Sir Ambrose Grange was out, he was informed, but he was expected back about six. Simon bought his evening paper, found that the favourite had won—he never backed favourites—and was at the telephone again when the hour struck.

"I'm taking you at your word and coming round to see you, Sir Ambrose."

"Delighted, my dear sir," said the knight, somewhat plaintively. "But if you'd told me I could have got hold of some girls—"

"Never mind the girls," said Simon.

He arrived at the lodgings in Seymour Street where Sir Ambrose maintained his modest bachelor *pied-a-terre* half an hour later, and plunged into his business without preliminaries.

"I've come to buy your Buddha," he said. "Two thousand was what your uncle wanted, wasn't it?"

Sir Ambrose goggled at him for some seconds; and then he laughed feebly.

"Ho, ho, ho! I bought that one, didn't I, by gad! Getting a bit slow on the uptake, what? Never mind, sir—have a drink."

"I'm not being comic," said the Saint. "I want your Buddha and I'll give you two thousand for it. I backed sixteen losers last week, and if I don't get a good mascot I shall be in the bankruptcy court."

After several minutes he was able to convince Sir Ambrose that his lunacy, if inexplicable, was backed up by a ready cheque-book. He wrote the figures with a flourish, and Sir Ambrose found himself fumbling for a piece of paper and a stamp to make out the receipt.

Simon read the document through—it was typical.

Received from Mr. Simon Templar, by cheque, the sum of Two Thousand Pounds, being payment for a brass Buddha which he knows is only worth fifteen shillings.

Ambrose Grange.

"Just to prove I knew what I was doing? I expected that."

Sir Ambrose looked at him suspiciously.

"I wish I knew what you wanted that thing for," he said. "Even my uncle only wanted us to get a thousand for it, but I thought I'd double it for luck. Two thousand couldn't be much more impossible than one." He heaved with chin-flivvering mirth. "Well, my dear sir, if you can make a profit on two thousand, I shan't complain. Ho, ho, ho, ho, ho! Have a drink."

"Sometimes," said the Saint quite affably, "I wonder why there's no law classifying men like you as vermin and authorising you to be sprayed with weed-killer on sight."

He routed out Peter Quentin before going home that night, and uttered the same philosophy to him —ever more affably. The brass Buddha sat on a table beside his bed when he turned in, and he blew it a kiss before he switched out the light and sank into the dreamless sleep of a contented corsair.

He paraded at the Savoy at twelve-thirty the next day.

At two o'clock Patricia Holm found him in the grill-room.

Simon beckoned the waiter who had just poured out his coffee, and asked for another cup.

"Well," he said, "where's Peter?"

"His girl friend stopped in a shop window to look at some stockings, so I came on." Her eyebrows were faintly questioning. "I thought you were lunching with that American.

Simon dropped two lumps of sugar in his cup and stirred it lugubriously.

"Pat," he said, "you may put this down in your notes for our textbook on Crime—the perfect confidence trick, Version Two. Let me tell you about it."

She lighted a cigarette slowly, staring at him.

"The Mug," said the Saint deliberately, "meets an Unpleasant Man. The Unpleasant Man purposely makes himself out to be so sharp that no normally healthy Mug could resist the temptation to do him down if the opportunity arose; and he may credit himself with a title just to remove all suspicion. The Unpleasant Man has something to sell—it might be a brass Buddha, valued at fifteen shillings, for which he's got to realise some fantastic sum like two thousand quid under the terms of an eccentric will. The Mug admits that the problem is difficult, and passes out into the night."

Simon annexed Patricia's cigarette, and inhaled from it.

"Shortly afterwards," he said, "the Mug meets the Nice American who is looking for a very special brass Buddha valued at fifteen thousand bucks. The Nice American gives away certain information which allows the Mug to perceive, beyond all possible doubt, that this rare and special Buddha is the very one for which the Unpleasant Man was trying to get what he thought was the fantastic price of two thousand quid. The Mug, therefore, with the whole works taken right down into his stomach—hook, line, and sinker—dashes round to the Unpleasant Man and gives him his two thousand quid. And he endorses a receipt saying he knows it's only worth fifteen bob, so that the Unpleasant Man can prove himself innocent of deception. Then the Mug goes to meet the Nice American and collect his profit. . . . And, Pat, I regret to say that he pays for his own lunch."

The Saint gazed sadly at the folded bill which a waiter had just placed on the table.

Patricia was wide-eyed.

"Simon! Did you—?"

"I did. I paid two thousand quid of our hard-won boodle to that perambulating sausage—"

He broke off, with his own jaw sinking.

James G. Amberson was flying across the room, with his Panama hat waving in his hand and his spectacles gleaming. He flung himself into a chair at the Saint's table.

"Say, did you think I was dead? My watch musta stopped while I was huntin' round junk stores in Limehouse—I saw a clock outa the taxi window as I was comin' back, and had a heart attack. Gosh, I'm sorry!"

"That's all right," murmured the Saint. "Pat, you haven't met Mr. Amberson. This is our Nice American. James G.—Miss Patricia Holm."

"Say, I'm real pleased to meet you, Miss Holm. Guess Mr. Templar told you how I fainted in his arms yesterday." Amberson reached over and wrung the girl's hand heartily. "Well, Mr. Templar, if you've had lunch you can have a liqueur." He waved to a waiter. "And, say, did you find me that Buddha?"

Simon bent down and hauled a small parcel out from under the table.

"This is it."

Amberson gaped at the package for a second; and then he grabbed it and tore it open. He gaped again at the contents—then at the Saint.

"Well, I'm a son of a—Excuse me, Miss Holm, but—"

"Is that right?" asked the Saint.

"I'll say it is!" Amberson was fondling the image as if it were his own long-lost child. "What did I promise you? Fifteen thousand berries?"

He pulled out his wallet and spilled American bills on to the table.

"Fifteen grand it is, Mr. Templar. And I guess I'm grateful. Mind if I leave you now? I gotta get on the transatlantic phone to Lou Froussard and tell him, and then I gotta rush this little precious into a safe deposit. Say, let me ring you up and invite you to a real dinner next week."

He shook hands again, violently, with Patricia and the Saint, caught up his Panama, and vomited out of the room again like a human whirligig.

In the vestibule a podgy and pompous little man with bushy mustachios was waiting for him. He seized James G. Amberson by the arm.

"Did you get it, Jim?"

"You bet I did!" Amberson exhibited his purchase. His excessively American speech had disappeared. "And now d'you mind telling me why we've bought it? I'm just packing up for our getaway when you rush me round here to spend fifteen thousand dollars—"

"I'll tell you how it was, Jim," said the other rapidly. "I'm sitting on top of a bus, and there's a man and a girl in front of me. The first thing I heard was 'Twenty thousand pounds' worth of black pearls in a brass Buddha.' I just had to listen. This chap seemed to be a solicitor's clerk, and he was telling his girl about an old miser who shoved these pearls into a brass Buddha after his wife died, and nobody found the letter where he said what he'd done till long after he was buried. 'And we've got to try and trace the thing,' says this young chap. 'It was sold to a junk dealer with a lot of other stuff, and heaven knows where it may be now.' 'How d'you know you've got it when you find it?' says the girl. 'Easy,' says this chap. 'It's got a mark on it like this.' He drew it on his paper, and I nearly broke my neck getting a look. Come on, now—let's get it home and open it."

"I hope Ambrose and James G. are having lots of fun looking for your black pearls, Peter," drawled the Saint piously, as he stood at the counter of Thomas Cook and watched American bills translating themselves into English bank-notes with a fluency that was all the heart could desire.

THE PERFECT CRIME

"The Defendants," said Mr. Justice Goldie, with evident distaste, "have been unable to prove that the agreement between the plaintiff and the late Alfred Green constituted a money-lending transaction within the limits of the Act; and I am therefore obliged to give judgment for the plaintiff. I will consider the question of costs to-morrow."

The Saint tapped Peter Quentin on the shoulder as the court rose, and they slipped out ahead of the scanty assembly of spectators, bored reporters, dawdling solicitors, and traditionally learned counsel. Simon Templar had sat in that stuffy little room for two hours, bruising his narrow-bones on an astonishingly hard wooden bench and yearning for a cigarette; but there were times when he could endure many discomforts in a good cause.

Outside, he caught Peter's arm again.

"Mind if I take another look at our plaintiff?" he said. "Just over here—stand in front of me. I want to see what a snurge like that really looks like."

They stood in a gloomy corner near the door of

the court, and Simon sheltered behind Peter Quentin's hefty frame and watched James Deever come out with his solicitor.

It is possible that Mr. Deever's mother loved him. Perhaps, holding him on her knee, she saw in his childish face the fulfilment of all those precious hopes and shy, incommunicable dreams which (if we can believe the *Little Mothers' Weekly*) are the joy and comfort of the prospective parent. History does not tell us that. But we do know that since her death, thirty years ago, no other bosom had ever opened to him with anything like that sublime mingling of pride and affection.

He was a long, cadaverous man with a face like a vulture and shaggy white eyebrows over closely set, greenish eyes. His thin nose swooped low down over a thin gash of a mouth, and his chin was pointed and protruding. In no respect whatsoever was it the kind of countenance to which young children take an instinctive shine. Grown men and women, who knew him, liked him even less.

His home and business address were in Manchester; but the City Corporation had never been heard to boast about it. Simon Templar watched him walk slowly past, discussing some point in the case he had just won with the air of a parson conferring with a churchwarden after matins, and the reeking hypocrisy of the performance filled him with an almost irresistible desire to catch Mr. Deever's frock-coated stern with the toe of his shoe and start him on one sudden, magnificent flight to the foot of the stairs. The Manchester City Corporation, Simon considered, could probably have kept their ends up without Mr. Deever's name on the roll of ratepayers. But the Saint restrained himself, and went on peaceably with Peter Quentin five minutes afterwards.

"Let us drink beer," said the Saint.

They entered a convenient tavern, lighting cigarettes as they went, and found a secluded corner in the saloon bar. The court had sat on late, and the hour had struck at which it is lawful for Englishmen to consume the refreshment which can only be bought at any time of the day in nasty, uncivilised foreign countries.

And for a few minutes there was silence. . . .

"It's wonderful what you can do with the full sanction of the law," Peter Quentin said presently, in a rather sourly reflective tone; and the Saint smiled at him wryly. He knew that Peter was not thinking about the more obvious inanities of the Defence of the Realm.

"I rather wanted to get a good close-up of James, and watch him in action," he said. "I guess all the stories are true."

There were several stories about James Deever; but none of them ever found their way into print—for libel actions mean heavy damages, and Mr. Deever sailed very comfortably within the law. His business was plainly and publicly that of a moneylender, and as a moneylender he was duly and legally registered according to the Act which has done so much to bring the profession of usury within certain humane restrictions. And as a plain and registered moneylender Mr. Deever retained his offices in Manchester, superintending every detail of his business in person, trusting nobody, sending out beautifully worded circulars in which he proclaimed his readiness to lend anybody any sum from £10 to £50,000 on note of hand alone, and growing many times richer than the Saint thought anyone but himself had any right to be. Nevertheless, Mr. Deever's business would probably have escaped the Saint's attentions if those few facts had covered the whole general principle of it.

They didn't. Mr. Deever, who, in spite of the tenor of his artistically printed circulars, was not in the moneylending business on account of any urge to go down to mythology as the little fairy godmother of Manchester, had devised half a dozen ingenious and strictly legal methods of evading the limitations placed on him by the Act. The prospective borrower who came to him, full of faith and hope, for the loan of £10 to £50,000 was frequently obliged—not, one must admit, on his note of hand alone, but eventually on the basis of some very sound security. And if the loan were promptly repaid, there the matter ended—at the statutory rate of interest for such transactions. It was only when the borrower found himself in further difficulties that Mr. Deever's ingenious schemes came into operation. It was then that his victim found himself straying little by little into a maze of complicated mortgages, discounted cheques, "nominal" promissory notes, mysterious "conversions," and technically worded transfers—straying into that labyrinth so gradually at first that it all seemed quite harmless, slipping deeper into it over an easy path of documents and signatures, floundering about in it at last and losing his bearings more and more hopelessly in his struggles to climb back—finally awakening to the haggard realisation that by some incomprehensible jugglery of papers and figures he owed Mr. Deever five or six times as much money as Mr. Deever had given him in cash, and having it

proved to him over his own signature that there
was no question of the statutory rate of interest
having been exceeded at any time.

Exactly thus had it been proved to the widow of
a certain victim in the case that they had listened to
that afternoon; and there were other similar cases
that had come to the Saint's receptive knowledge.

"There were days," remarked the Saint, rather
wistfully, "when some lads of the village and I
would have carved Brother Deever into small
pieces and baited lobster-pots with him from the
North Foreland to the Lizard."

"And what now?" queried Peter Quentin.

"Now," said the Saint, regretfully, "we can only
call on him for a large involuntary contribution to
our Pension Fund for Deserving Outlaws."

Peter lowered the first quarter of his second pint.

"It'll have to be something pretty smart to catch
that bird," he said. "If you asked me, I should say
you couldn't take any story to him that wouldn't
have to pass under a microscope."

"For which reason," murmured Simon Templar,
with the utmost gravity, "I shall go to him with a
story that is absolutely true. I shall approach him
with a hook and line that the cleverest detective on
earth couldn't criticise. You're right, Peter—there
probably isn't a swindle in the encyclopaedia that
would get a yard past Brother James. It's a good
thing we aren't criminals, Pete—we might get our
fingers burned. No, laddie. Full of righteousness
and the stuff that passes for beer in this country, we
shall draw nigh to Brother James with four haloes
fairly glistening. It was just for a man like him that
I was saving up my Perfect Crime."

If the Saint's halo was not actually visibly luminous when he called at Mr. Deever's offices the next morning, he at least looked remarkably harmless. A white flower ("for purity," said the Saint) started in his button-hole and flowed in all directions over his coat lapel; a monocle was screwed into his right eye; his hat sat precariously on the back of his head; and his face was relaxed into an expression of such amiably aristocratic idiocy that Mr. Deever's chief clerk—a man hardly less sour-visaged than Mr. Deever himself—was even more obsequious than usual.

Simon said he wanted a hundred pounds, and would cheerfully give a jolly old note of hand for it if some johnnie would explain to him what a jolly old note of hand was. The clerk explained, oleaginously, that a jolly old note of hand was a somewhat peculiar sort of thing that sounded nice in advertisements, but wasn't really used with important clients. Had Mr.—er—Smith?—had Mr. Smith any other kind of security?

"I've got some jolly old premium bonds," said the Saint; and the clerk nodded his head in a perfect sea of oil.

"If you can wait a moment, sir, perhaps Mr. Deever will see you himself."

The Saint had no doubt that Mr. Deever would see him. He waited around patiently for a few minutes, and was ushered into Mr. Deever's private sanctum.

"You see, I lost a bally packet at Derby yesterday—every blinkin' horse fell down dead when I backed it. I work a system, but of course you can't back a winner every day. I know I'll get it back, though—the chappie who sold me the system said it had never let him down."

Mr. Deever's eyes gleamed. If there was any-thing that satisfied every one of his requirements for a successful loan, it was an asinine young man with a monocle who believed in racing systems.

"I believe you mentioned some security, Mr.—er —Smith. Naturally we should be happy to lend you a hundred pounds without any formalities, but—"

"Oh, I've got these jolly old bonds. I don't want to sell 'em, because they're having a draw this month. If you hold the lucky number you get a fat bonus. Sort of lottery business, but quite gilt-edged an' all that sort of thing."

He produced a large envelope, and passed it across Mr. Deever's desk. Deever extracted a bunch of expensively watermarked papers artisti-cally engraved with green and cold lettering which proclaimed them to be Latvian 1929 Premium Loan (British Series) Bearer Bonds, value £25 each.

The financier crunched them between his fingers, squinted at the ornate characters suspicously through a magnifying glass, and looked again at the Saint.

"Of course, Mr. Smith, we don't keep large sums of money on the premises. But if you like to leave these bonds with me until, say, two o'clock this af-ternoon, I'm sure we shall be able to make a satis-factory arrangement."

"Keep 'em by every manner of means, old bean," said the Saint airily. "So long as I get the jolly old quidlets in time to take 'em down to the three-thirty to-day, you're welcome."

Conveniently enough, this happened to be the first day of the Manchester September meeting. Si-mon Templar paraded again at two o'clock, col-

lected his hundred pounds, and rejoined Peter
Quentin at their hotel.

"I have a hundred pounds of Brother James's
money," he announced. "Let's go and spread it
around on the most frantic outsiders we can find."

They went to the races, and it so happened that
the Saint's luck was in. He had doubled Mr.
Deever's hundred pounds when the result of the
last race went up on the board—but Mr. Deever
would not have been seriously troubled if he had
lost the lot. Five hundred pounds worth of Latvian
Bearer Bonds had been deposited as security for
the advance, and in spite of the artistic engraving
on them there was no doubt that they were genuine. The interval between Simon Templar's visit to
Mr. Deever in the morning and the time when the
money was actually paid over to him had been devoted to an expert scrutiny of the bonds, coupled
with inquiries at Mr. Deever's brokers, which had
definitely established their authenticity—and the
Saint knew it.

"I wonder," Simon Templar was saying as they
drove back into the town, "if there's any place here
where you could buy a false beard. With all this
money in our pockets, why should you wait for
Nature to take her course?"

Nevertheless, it was not with the air of a man
who had collected a hundred pounds over a couple
of well-chosen winners that the Saint came to Mr.
Deever the next day. It was Saturday, but that
meant nothing to Mr. Deever. He was a man who
kept only the barest minimum of holidays, and
much good business might be done with temporarily embarrassed members of the racing fraternity on
the second day of the meeting.

It appeared very likely on this occasion.

"I don't know how the horse managed to lose," said the Saint mournfully.

"Dear me!" said Mr. Deever unctuously. "Dear me! Did it lose?"

The Saint nodded.

"I don't understand it at all. The chappie who sold me this system said it had never had more than three losers in succession. And the stakes go up so frightfully fast. You see, you have to put on more money each time, so that when you win you get back your losses as well. But it simply must win to-day—'"

"How much do you need to put on to-day, Mr. Smith?"

"About eight hundred pounds. But what with buzzing around an' having a few drinks and what not, don't you know—if you could make it an even thou—"

Mr. Deever rubbed his hands over each other with a face of abysmal gloom.

"A thousand pounds is quite a lot of money, Mr. —er—Smith, but of course if you can offer some security—purely as a business formality, you understand—"

"Oh, I've got lots more of those jolly old Latvian Bonds," said the Saint. "I think I bought about two hundred of 'em. Got to try and pick up a bonus somehow, what?"

Mr. Deever nodded like a mandarin.

"Of course, Mr. Smith. Of course. And it just happens that one of our advances was repaid to-day, so I may be able to find a thousand pounds for you in our safe." He pressed a bell on his desk, and a clerk appeared. "Mr. Goldberg, will you see if we can oblige this gentleman with a thousand pounds?''

The clerk disappeared again, and came back in a few moments with a sheaf of bank-notes. Simon Templar produced another large envelope, and Mr. Deever drew from it an even thicker wad of bonds. He counted them over and examined them carefully one by one; then he took a printed form from a drawer, and unscrewed the cap of a Woolworth fountain-pen.

"Now if you will just complete our usual agreement, Mr. Smith—"

Through the glass partition that divided Mr. Deever's sanctum from the outer office there suddenly arose the expostulations of an extraordinarily loud voice. Raised in a particularly raucous north-country accent, it made itself heard so clearly that there was no chance of missing anything it said.

"I tell you, I'd know thaat maan anywhere. I'd know'im in a daark room if I was bliindfooalded. It *was* Simon Templar, I tell you. I saw 'im coom in, an' I says to myself, 'Thaat's Saaint, thaat is.' I 'aad wife an' loogage with me, so I taakes 'em into 'otel an' cooms straight baack. I'm going to see thaat Saaint if I waait here two years—"

The buttery voice of Mr. Goldberg could be heard protesting. Then the north-country voice drowned it again.

"Then if you won't let me in, I'll go straaight out an' fetch policeman. Thaat's what I'll do."

There was an eruption without, as of someone departing violently into the street; and the Saint looked at Mr. Deever. Simon's hand was outstretched to grasp the pile of banknotes—then he saw Deever's right hand come out of a drawer, and a nickel-plated revolver with it.

"Just a moment, Mr.—er—Smith," Deever said slowly. "I think you're in too much of a hurry."

He touched the bell on his desk again. Mr. Goldberg reappeared, mopping his swarthy brow. There was a glitter in Deever's greenish eyes which told Simon that the revolver was not there merely for the purposes of intimidation. The Saint sat quite still.

"Look in this gentleman's pockets, Mr. Goldberg. Perhaps he has some evidence of identity on him."

The clerk came over and began a search. The monocle had vanished from the Saint's right eye, and the expression on his face was anything but vacuous.

"You filthy miser!" he blazed. "I'll see that you're sorry for this. No one has insulted me like this for years—"

Coolly Deever leaned over the desk and smacked Simon over the mouth. The blow cut the Saint's lip.

"A crook should be careful of his tongue," Deever said.

"There's a letter here, Mr. Deever," said the clerk, laying it on the blotter. "It's addressed to Simon Templar. And I found this as well."

"This," was another large envelope, the exact replica of the one in which Simon had handed over his Latvian Bonds. Deever opened it, and found that it contained a similar set of bonds; and when he had counted them he found that they were equal in number to those which he had accepted for security.

"I see, Mr.—er—Smith." The close-set eyes gloated. "So I've been considered worthy of the attentions of the famous Saint. And a very pretty swindle too. First you borrow money on some more genuine bonds; then you come back and try to borrow more money on some more genuine bonds—but when I'm not looking you exchange them for forgeries. Very neat, Mr. Templar. It's a pity that man outside recognised you. Mr. Goldberg, I think you might telephone for the police."

"You'll be sorry for this," said the Saint more calmly, with his eyes on Deever's revolver.

A police inspector arrived in a few minutes. He inspected the two envelopes, and nodded.

"That's an old trick, Mr. Deever," he said. "It's lucky that you were warned. Come along, you—put your hands out."

"You don't need those," he said.

"I've heard about you," said the inspector grimly, "and I think we do. Come on, now, and no nonsense."

For the first time in his life Simon felt the cold embrace of steel on his wrists. A constable put his hat on for him, and he was marched out into the street. A small crowd had collected outside, and already the rumour of his identity was passing from mouth to mouth.

The local inspector did not spare him. Simon Templar was a celebrity, a capture that every officer in England had once dreamed of making, even if of late it had been found impossible to link his name with any proven crimes; and once arrested he was an exhibit to be proud of. The police station was not far away, and the Saint was compelled to walk to it, with his manacled wrists chained to the burly constable on his left and the inspector striding on his right.

He was charged with attempting to obtain money under false pretences; and when it was all written down they asked him if he had anything to say.

"Only that my right sock is wearing a bit thin at the heel," answered the Saint. "D'you think someone could beetle along to my hotel and dig out a new pair?"

He was locked in a cell to be brought before the magistrate on the following Monday. It was Simon Templar's third experience of that, but he enjoyed it no more than the first time.

During Sunday he had one consolation. He was able to divert himself with thoughts of what he could do with about ten thousand pounds.

Monday morning brought a visitor to Manchester in the portly shape of Chief Inspector Claud Eustace Teal, who automatically came north at the news of the sensational arrest which had been the front-page splash of every newspaper in the kingdom. But the expert witness who came with him caused a much greater sensation. He examined the contents of the two envelopes, and scratched his head.

"Is this a joke?" he demanded. "Every one of these bonds is perfectly genuine. There isn't a forgery among them."

The local inspector's eyes popped half-way out of his head.

"Are you sure?" he blurted.

"Of course I'm sure," snapped the disgusted expert. "Any fool can see that with half an eye. Did

I have to give up a perfectly good day's golf to tell you that?"

Chief Inspector Teal was not interested in the expert's golf. He sat on a bench and held his head in his hands. He was not quite certain how it had been worked, but he knew there was something very wrong somewhere.

Presently he looked up.

"And Deever struck him in the office—that isn't denied?"

"No, sir," admitted the local inspector. "Mr. Deever said—"

"And you marched Templar through the streets in broad daylight, handcuffed to a constable?"

"Yes, sir. Knowing what I did about him—"

"I'd better see the Saint," said Teal. "If I'm not mistaken, someone's going to be sorry they knew so much."

He was shown into Simon's cell, and the Saint rose languidly to greet him.

"Hullo, Claud," he murmured. "I'm glad you've arrived. A gang of these local half-wits in funny hats—"

"Never mind that," said Teal bluntly. "Tell me what you're getting out of this."

Simon pondered.

"I shouldn't accept anything less than ten thousand pounds," he said finally.

The light in Chief Inspector Teal's understanding strengthened slowly. He turned to the local inspector, who had accompanied him.

"By the way," he said, "I suppose you never found that man from Huddersfield, or whoever it was that blew the gaff?"

"No, sir. We've made inquiries at all the hotels,

but he seems to have disappeared. I've got a sort of description of him—a fairly tall, broad-shouldered man with a beard—"

"I see," said Teal, very sleepily.

Simon dipped into the local inspector's pocket and calmly borrowed a packet of cigarettes. He lighted one.

"If it's any help to you," he said, "the report of everything that happened in Deever's office is perfectly true. I went to see him for some money, and then I went to him for some more. Every time I offered excellent security. I behaved myself like a law-abiding citizen—"

"Why did you call yourself Smith?"

"Why shouldn't I? It's a grand old English name. And I always understood that you could call yourself anything you liked so long as you didn't do it with intent to defraud. Go and tell Deever to prove the fraud. I just had to have some cash to go to the races, I had those Latvian Bonds with me, and I thought that if I gave my real name I'd be making all sorts of silly difficulties. That's all there was to it. But did anyone make an honest attempt to find out if there was a fraud?"

"I see," said Teal again—and he really did see.

"They did not," said the Saint in a pained voice. "What happened? I was assaulted. I was abused. I was handcuffed and marched through the streets like a common burglar, followed by shop girls and guttersnipes, snapped by press photographers. I was shoved in a cell for forty-eight hours, and I wasn't even allowed to send for a clean pair of socks. A bunch of flat-footed nincompoops told me when to get up, when to eat, when to take exercise, and when to go to bed again—just as if I'd already been convicted. Deever's story has been published in every paper in the United Kingdom. And d'you know what that means?"

Teal did not answer. And the Saint's forefinger tapped him just where his stomach began to bulge, tapped him debonairly in the rhythm of the Saint's seraphic accents, in a gesture that Teal knew only too well.

"It means that there's one of the swellest legal actions on earth waiting for me to win it—an action for damages for wrongful imprisonment, defamation of character, libel, slander, assault, battery, and the Lord alone knows what not. I wouldn't take a penny less than ten thousand pounds. I may even want more. And do you think James Deever won't come across?"

Chief Inspector Teal had no reply. He knew Deever would pay.

THE UNPOPULAR LANDLORD

There were periods in Simon Templar's eventful life when that insatiable wanderlust which had many times sent him half-way round the world on fantastic quests that somehow never materialised in quite the way they had been intended to, invaded even his busy life in London. He became bored with looking out on to the same street scene from his windows every day, or he saw some other domicile on the market which appealed to his catholic taste in residences, or else he moved because he thought that too long an interval of stability would weaken his resistance to regular hours and *Times*-reading and other low forms of human activity. At these periods he would change his address with such frequency that his friends despaired of ever establishing contact with him again. It was one of the few aimless things he did; and it never provided any exciting sequels—except on this one historic occasion which the chronicler has to record.

Simon Templar awoke on this particular morning with that familiar feeling of restlessness upon him; and, having nothing else of importance to distract him that day, he sallied forth to interview an estate agent. This interviewing of estate agents is a business that is quite sufficient to discourage any migratory urges which may afflict the average man; but Simon Templar had become inured to it over the course of years. He sought out the offices of Messrs. Potham & Spode, obtained the services of Mr. Potham, and prepared to be patient.

Mr. Potham was a thin, angular man with grey hair, gold-rimmed spectacles, and a face that receded in progressive stages from his eyebrows to the base of his neck. He was a harmless man enough, kind to his children and faithful to his wife, a man whose income tax returns were invariably honest to the uttermost farthing; but twenty years of his profession had had their inevitable effect.

"I want," said the Saint distinctly, "an unfurnished non-service flat, facing south or west, with four large rooms, and a good, open outlook, at not more than five hundred a year."

Mr. Potham rummaged through a large file, and eventually, with an air of triumph, drew forth a sheet.

"Now here," he said, "I think we have the very thing you're looking for. No. 101, Park Lane: one bedroom, one reception-room—"

"Making four rooms," murmured the Saint patiently.

Mr. Potham peered at him over the rims of his glasses and sighed. He replaced the sheet carefully, and drew forth another.

"Now this," he said, "seems to suit all your requirements. There are two bed, two reception, kitchen and bath; and the rent is extremely moderate. Our client is actually paying fifteen hundred a year, exclusive of rates; but in order to secure a quick let he is ready to pass on the lease at the very reasonable rent of twelve hundred—"

"I said five hundred," murmured the Saint.

Mr. Potham turned back to his file with a hurt expression.

"Now here, Mr. Templar," he said, "we have No. 27, Cloudesley Street, Berkeley Square—"

"Which faces north," murmured the Saint.

"Does it?" said Mr. Potham, in some pain.

"I'm afraid it does," said the Saint ruthlessly. "All the odd numbers in Cloudesley Street do."

Mr. Potham put back the sheet with the air of an adoring mother removing her offspring from the vicinity of some stranger who had wantonly smacked it. He searched through his file for some time before he produced his next offering.

"Well, Mr. Templar," he said, adjusting his spectacles rather nervously, "I have here a very charming service flat—"

Simon Templar knew from bitter experience that this process could be prolonged almost indefinitely; but that day he had one or two helpful ideas.

"I saw a flat to let as I came along here—just round the corner, in David Square," he said. "It looked like the sort of thing I'm wanting, from the outside."

"David Square?" repeated Mr. Potham, frowning. "I don't think I know of anything there."

"It had a Potham and Spode board hung out," said the Saint relentlessly. "Perhaps Spode hung it up one dark night when you weren't looking."

"David Square!" re-echoed Mr. Potham, like a forsaken bass in an oratorio. "David Square!" He polished his spectacles agitatedly, burrowed into his file again, and presently looked up over his gold rims. "Would that be No. 17?"

"I think it would."

Mr. Potham extracted the page of particulars and leaned back, gazing at the Saint with a certain tinge of pity.

"There is a flat to let at No. 17, David Square," he admitted in a hushed voice, as if he were reluctantly discussing a skeleton in his family cupboard. "It is one of Major Bellingford Smart's buildings."

He made this announcement as though he expected the Saint to recoil from it with a cry of horror, and looked disappointed when the cry did not come. But the Saint pricked up his ears. Mr. Potham's tone, and the name of Bellingford Smart, touched a dim chord of memory in his mind; and never in his life had one of those chords let the Saint astray. Somewhere, some time, he knew that he had heard the name of Bellingford Smart before, and it had not been in a complimentary reference.

"What's the matter with that?" he asked coolly. "Is he a leper or something?"

Mr. Potham smoothed down the sheet on his blotter with elaborate precision.

"Major Bellingford Smart," he said judiciously, "is not a landlord with whose property we are anxious to deal. We have it on our books, since he sends us particulars; but we don't offer it unless we are specially asked for it."

"But what does he do?" persisted the Saint.

"He is—ah-somewhat difficult to get on with," replied Mr. Potham cautiously.

More than that his discretion would not permit him to say; but the Saint's appetite was far from satisfied. In fact, Simon Templar was so intrigued with the unpopularity of Major Bellingford Smart that he took his leave of Mr. Potham rather abruptly, leaving that discreet gentleman gaping in some astonishment at a virginal pad of Orders to View on which he had not been given a chance to inscribe any addresses for the Saint's inspection.

Simon Templar was not actively in search of trouble at that time. His hours of meditation, as a matter of fact, were almost exclusively occupied with the problem of devising for himself an effective means of entering the town house of the Countess of Albury (widow of Albury's Peerless Pickles) whose display of diamonds at a recent public function had impressed him as being a potential contribution to his Old Age Pension that he could not conscientiously pass by. But one of those sudden impulses of his had decided that the time was ripe for knowing more about Major Bellingford Smart; and in such a mood as that, a comparatively straightforward proposition like the Countess of Albury's diamonds had to take second place.

Simon went along to a more modern estate agency than the honourable firm of Potham & Spode, one of those marble-pillared, super-card-index billeting offices where human habitations are shot at you over the counter like sausages in a cafeteria; and there an exquisitely dressed young man with a double-breasted waistcoat and hair even more impossibly patent-leather than the Saint's own, who looked as if he could have been nothing less than the second son of a duke or an ex-motor-salesman, was more communicative than Mr. Potham had been. It is also worthy of note that the exquisite young man thought that he was volunteering the information quite spontaneously, as a matter of interest to an old friend of his youth; for the Saint's tact and guile could be positively Machiavellian when he chose.

"It's rather difficult to say exactly what *is* the matter with Bellingford Smart. He seems to be one of these sneaking swine who get pleasure out of taking advantage of their position in petty ways. As far as his tenants are concerned, he keeps to the letter of his leases and makes himself as nasty as possible within those limits. There are lots of ways a landlord can make life unbearable for you if he wants to, as you probably know. The people he likes to get into his flats are lonely widows and elderly spinsters—they're easy meat for him."

"But I don't see what good that does him," said the Saint puzzledly. "He's only getting himself a bad name—"

"I had one of his late tenants in here the other day—she told me that she'd just paid him five hundred pounds to release her. She couldn't stand it any longer, and she couldn't get out any other way. If he does that often, I suppose it must pay him."

"But he's making it more and more difficult to let his flats, isn't he?"

The exquisite young man shrugged.

"All the estate agencies know him—we refuse to handle his stuff at all, and we aren't the only ones. But there are plenty of prospective tenants who've never heard of him. He advertises his flats and lets them himself whenever he can, and then the tenants don't find out their mistake till it's too late. It must seem amazing to you that anything like that can go on in this neighbourhood; but his petty persecutions are all quite legal, and nobody seems to be able to do anything about it."

"I see," said the Saint softly.

The solution of the mystery, now that he knew it, struck him as being one of the most original, and at the same time one of the meanest and most contemptible, forms of blackmail that he had ever heard of; and the fact that it skulked along under the cover of the law made it twice as sickening. He had no doubt that it was all true—even the worthiest of estate agents are not in the habit of turning down commissions without the strongest possible grounds, and Major Bellingford Smart's nastiness appeared to be common knowledge in the profession. There were some forms of unpleasantness that filled the Saint with an utter loathing, and the meanness of Major Bellingford Smart was one of them. Simon had an entirely immoral respect for the whole-hearted criminal who gambled his liberty on the success of his enterprises, but a livelihood that was gained principally by bullying and swindling fat-headed old women turned his stomach.

"He had quite a lot of property around here," the exquisite young man was informing him. "He buys up houses and converts them into flats. You'll see what sort of a man he is when I tell you that while his conversions are being carried out it's his habit to hire a room in the neighbourhood from which he can overlook the site, and he prowls around there at odd times with a pair of field-glasses to see if he can catch his workmen slacking. Once he saw a couple of men having a cup of tea in the afternoon, and went round and fired them on the spot."

"Isn't there anything he doesn't sink to?" asked the Saint.

"I can't think of it," said the exquisite young

man slanderously. "A few months ago he had a porter at 17, David Square who'd stayed with him eleven years—I can't think why. The porter's wife acted as a sort of housekeeper, and their daughter was employed in the Major's own flat as a maid. You can imagine what a man like that must be like to work for, and this daughter soon found she couldn't stick it. She tried to give notice, and Smart told her that if she left him her father and mother would be fired out into the street—the porter was an old man of well over sixty. The girl tried to stay on, but at last she had to run away. The first the porter and his wife knew about it was when Smart sent for them and gave them a month's notice. And at the end of the month they duly were fired out, with Smart still owing them three weeks' wages which they tried for weeks to get out of him until the son of one of the tenants went round and saw Smart and damned well made him pay up under the threat of putting his own solicitors on the job. The porter died shortly afterwards. I expect it all sounds incredible, but it's quite true."

Simon departed with a sheaf of Orders to View which he destroyed as soon as he got outside, and walked round very thoughtfully in the direction of David Square. And the more he thought of it, the more poisonous and utterly septic the personality of Major Bellingford Smart loomed in his consciousness. It occurred to the Saint, with a certain honest regret, that the calls of his own breezy buccaneering had lately taken his thoughts too far from that unlawful justice which had once made his name a terror more salutary than the Law to those who sinned secretly in tortuous ways that the Law could not touch. And it was very pleasant to think that the old life was still open to him. . . .

With those thoughts he sauntered up the steps of No. 17, where he was stopped by a uniformed porter who looked more like a prison warder—which, as a matter of fact, he had once been.

"Can you tell me anything about this flat that's to let here?" Simon inquired, and the man's manner changed.

"You'd better see Major Bellingford Smart, sir. Will you step this way?"

Simon was led round to an extraordinarily gloomy and untidy office on the ground floor, where a man who was writing at a desk littered with dust-smothered papers rose and nodded to him.

"You want to see the flat, Mr.—er—"

"Bourne," supplied the Saint. "Captain Bourne."

"Well, Captain Bourne," said the Major dubiously, "I hardly know whether it would be likely to suit you. As a matter of fact—"

"It doesn't have to suit me," said the Saint expansively. "I'm inquiring about it for my mother. She's a widow, you know, and she isn't very strong. Can't go walking around London all day looking at flats. I have to go back to India myself at the end of the week, and I very much wanted to see the old lady fixed up before I sailed."

"Ah," said the Major, more enthusiastically, "that alters the situation. I was going to say that this flat would be quite ideal for an old lady living alone."

Simon was astounded once again at the proven simplicity of womankind. Major Bellingford Smart's transparent sliminess fairly assaulted him with nausea. He was a man of about forty-five, with black hair, closely set eyes, and a certain stiff-necked poise to his head that gave him a slightly sinister appearance when he moved. It seemed almost unbelievable that anyone could ever have been taken in by such an obvious excrescence; but the fact remained that many victims had undoubtedly fallen into his net.

"Would you like to see it?" suggested the Major.

Simon registered a mental biographical note that Bellingford Smart's military rank must have been won well out of sight of the firing line. If that Major had ever gone over the top he would certainly have perished from a mysterious bullet in the back —such accidents have happened to unpopular officers before.

The Saint said that he would like to see the flat, and Bellingford Smart personally escorted him up to it. It was not at all a bad flat, with good, large rooms overlooking the green oasis of the square; and Simon was unable to find fault with it. This was nice for him; for he would have offered no criticism even if the roof had been leaking and the wainscoting had been perforated with rat-holes till it looked like a colander.

"I believe this is the very thing I've been looking for," he said; and Major Bellingford Smart lathered his hands with invisible soap.

"I'm sure Mrs. Bourne would be very comfortable here," he said greasily. "I do everything I can to make my tenants feel thoroughly at home. I'm on the premises myself all day, and if she wanted any help I'd always be delighted to give it. The rest is as moderate as I can make it—only three hundred and fifty per annum, including rates."

Simon nodded.

"That seems quite reasonable," he said. "I'll tell my mother about it and see what she says."

"I'll show her round myself at any time she likes to call," said Bellingford Smart cordially. "I don't want to hurry you in any way," he added, as they were going down in the lift, "but for your own sake I ought to mention that I've already shown another lady the flat to-day, and I'm expecting to hear her decision in a day or two."

At any other time that hoary old bait would have evoked nothing more than one of the Saint's most silent razzberries; but that morning he felt very polite. His face assumed the correct expression of thinly veiled alarm which attacks the veteran house-hunter's features when he visualises his prize being snatched away from under his nose.

"I'll let you know definitely some time this evening," he said.

The Saint's patience and caution could be infinite when he felt that way; but there were other times when he felt that to pass over the iron whilst it was hot was a crime that would lay heavily on his conscience, and this was one of them. His sense of the poetry of buccaneering demanded that the retribution which he had devised for Major Bellingford Smart should strike swiftly; and he spent that afternoon on a tour of various shipping offices with no other idea in his mind. The Countess of Albury's diamonds crawled in second by several lengths. It meant taking risks of which in a less indignant mood he would never have been guilty; for

Simon Templar had made it a rule in life never to attack without knowing every inch of the ground and the precise density of every tuft of grass behind which he might want to take cover; but the strafing of Major Bellingford Smart was a duty that could not be delayed for that.

Nevertheless, he did take certain elementary precautions, as a result of which three well-dressed and subtly dependable-looking men gathered in the apartment of one of their number and slaked their thirsts with beer which the Saint had provided. This was at six o'clock.

The apartment was rented by Peter Quentin; and the other two were Roger Conway and Monty Hayward, who had been summoned by urgent telephone calls by a man whom they had not seen for many months.

"It seems years since I called out the Old Guard, souls," said the Saint, glancing at Roger and Monty. "But this is one evening when your little Simon has need of you."

"What's it all about?" asked Monty expectantly; and Simon drained his glass and told them as briefly as he could about the leprousness of Major Bellingford Smart.

"But," said the Saint, "I am about to afflict him with much sorrow; and that's where you stiffs come in. We are going to settle down to a stag party. Peter, your janitor saw me come in, and at about a quarter to ten we shall send for him and bribe him to go out and buy us some more beer—which will give him another chance to observe that I'm still here. But as soon as he's brought the beer, which I'm afraid I shall have to leave you toughs to drink, I shall hop nimbly out of the window on to the roofs below, descend smartly to the area at the back, proceed thence to the street, and go about my business, returning in about an hour by the same route. As soon as I'm in, we shall ring for the janitor again and demand further supplies of beer. He will replay that it's past closing time, and there will be some argument in which I shall play a prominent part—thereby establishing the fact that we have been together the whole jolly evening. And so we shall. We shall have been playing bridge steadily all the while, and there will be four markers all filled up with the identical scores to prove it—in addition to your solemn oaths. Do you get me?"

"What is this?" asked Roger Conway. "An alibi?"

"No more and no less, old dear," answered the Saint seraphically. "I spend this afternoon wading through passenger lists, and discovered that there actually is a Captain Bourne sailing on the *Otranto* from Tilbury at seven o'clock to-night, which saved me the trouble and expense of booking a passage in that name myself. So when Major Bellingford Smart tries to put over his story it will indubitably receive the polite ha-ha. You soaks are just here in case the episode comes to the ears of Claud Eustace Teal and he tries to work me into it."

Roger Conway shrugged rather ruefully.

"You're on, of course," he said. "But I wish there was more action in it."

Simon looked at him with a smile; for those two had shared many adventures in the old days, as also more recently had Monty Hayward; and he knew that both men sometimes looked back a trifle wistfully on those days out of the respectable surroundings that had subsequently engulfed them.

"Perhaps we may work together again before we die, Roger," he said.

Monty Hayward had another suggestion.

"What are you going to do to Bellingford Smart? Couldn't we all go after him and tar and feather him, or something?"

"I don't think so," said the Saint carefully. "You see, that would be against the Law, and these days I'm developing quite an agile technique for strafing the ungodly by strictly legal means."

His method in this case was not so unimpeachably legal as it might have been; but the Saint had a superb breadth of vision that was superior to such trivial details. At half-past six the most unpopular landlord in London received a telephone call.

"Is that Mr. Shark?" asked the Saint innocently.

"This is Major Bellingford Smart speaking," admitted the landlord, shaking the receiver at his end, which did not seem to be working very well. In any case, he was rather particular about being given his full appellation. "Who is that?"

"This is Captain Bourne. You remember I saw your flat this morning? . . . Well, I've had urgent orders to get back as quickly as possible, and I've had to change my plans. I'm catching the *Otranto* at midnight."

"Are you really?" said Major Bellingford Smart.

"I've told my mother all about the flat, and she seems to think it would suit her down to the ground. She's decided to take it on my recommendation; so if it's still available—"

"Oh, yes, the flat is still available," said Major

Bellingford Smart eagerly. "If Mrs. Bourne could call round any time to-morrow—"

"I rather wanted to see her settled before I left," said the Saint. "Naturally my time's rather limited, having to pack up in a rush like this, and I'm afraid I've several engagements to get through. I don't know if you could possibly call round here about half-past ten—you could bring the lease with you, so that I could go through it—and my mother would sign it to-night."

Major Bellingford Smart had arranged to go to a theatre that evening; but the theatre would still be there the next day. And suitable tenants were becoming considerably harder to find than they had been.

"Certainly I'll come round at half-past ten, if that'll help you at all, Captain Bourne. What is the address?"

"Number eight-o-one, Belgrade Square," said the Saint, and rang off happily.

Major Bellingford Smart was punctual if he was nothing else. It was exactly half-past ten when he arrived in Belgrade Square, and Simon Templar himself opened the door to him as he came up the steps.

"I'm afraid we're having a bit of trouble with the lights,' remarked the Saint genially. "The hall light's just fizzled out. Can you see your way into the sitting-room?"

He had an electric torch in his hand, and with it he lighted Major Bellingford Smart into the nearest room. Bellingford Smart heard him clicking the switch up and down, and cursing under his breath.

"Now this one's gone on strike, Major. I'm awfully sorry. Will you take the torch and make yourself at home while I go and look at the fuses? There's a decanter over in the corner—help yourself."

He bumped into Bellingford Smart in the darkness, recovered his balance, apologised, and thrust his flashlight into the Major's hand. The door closed behind him.

Major Bellingford Smart turned the beam of the torch round the room in search of a chair—and, possibly, the decanter referred to. In another second he was not thinking of either, for in one corner the circle of light splashed over a safe whose door hung drunkenly open, half separated from its hinges: lowering the beam a trifle, he saw an array of gleaming tools spread out on the floor beside it.

He gasped, and instinctively moved over to investigate. Outside in the hall he heard the crash of a brass tray clattering on the floor, and straightened up with a start. Then heavy feet came pounding along the passage, the door burst open, and the lights were switched on. The hall lights outside were also on—nothing seemed to be the matter with them. For a few moments they dazzled him; and then, when he had blinked the glare out of his eyes, he saw that the doorway was filled by a black-trousered butler, with his coat off, and a footman with his tunic half buttoned. They looked at him, then at the open safe, and then back at him again; and there was no friendliness in their eyes.

"Ho," said the butler at length, appearing to swell visibly. "So that's hit. Caught in the very hact, eh?"

"What the devil do you mean?" spluttered Major Bellingford Smart. "I came here at Captain Bourne's invitation to see Mrs. Bourne—"

"Not 'alf you didn't," said the butler austerely. "There ain't no Mrs. Bourne 'ere, and never 'as been. This is the Countess of Halbury's 'ouse, and you don't 'ave to tell me what you are." He turned to the footman. "James, you go hout and fetch a copper, quick. I can look hafter this bloke. Just let 'im try something!"

He commenced to roll up his right sleeve, with an anticipatory glint in his eye. He was a very large butler, ever so much larger than Major Bellingford Smart, and he looked as if he would like nothing better than a show of violence. Even the best butlers must yearn sometimes for the simple human pleasure of pushing their fists into a face that offends them.

"You'll be sorry for this," fumed Major Bellingford Smart impotently. "If this is the Countess of Halbury's house there must be some mistake—"

"Ho, yes," said the butler pleasantly. "There his a mistake, and you made it."

There followed a brief interval of inhospitable silence, until the footman returned with a constable in tow.

"There 'e is," announced the footman; but the butler quelled him with a glance.

"Hofficer," he said majestically, "we 'ave just caught this person red-'anded in the hact of burgling the 'ouse. 'Er ladyship is at present hout dining with Lady Hexmouth. 'Earing the sound of footsteps, we thought 'er ladyship 'ad returned, halthaough James remarked that it was not 'er ladyship's custom to let 'erself hin. Then we 'eard a crash as if the card tray in the 'all 'ad been hupset, and we noticed that the lights were hout, so we came along to see what it was."

"I can explain everything, officer," interrupted Major Bellingford Smart. "I was asked to come here to get a Mrs. Bourne's signature to the lease of a flat—"

"You was, was you?" said the constable, who had ambitions of making his mark in the C.I.D. at some future date. "Well, show me the lease."

Major Bellingford Smart felt in his pocket, and a sudden wild look came into his eyes. The lease which he had brought with him was gone; but there was something else there—something hard and knobbly.

The constable did not miss that change of expression. He came closer to Major Bellingford Smart.

"Come on, now," he ordered rougly. "Out with it—whatever it is. And no monkey business."

Slowly, stupidly, Major Bellingford Smart drew out the hard knobbly object. It was a very small automatic, and looped loosely round it was a diamond and sapphire pendant—one of the least valuable items in the Countess of Albury's vanished collection. He was still staring at it when the constable grabbed it quickly out of his hand.

"Carrying firearms, eh? And that talk about 'aving a lease in your pocket—just to get a chance to pull it out and shoot me! You've got it coming to you, all right."

He glanced round the room with a professional air, and saw the open window.

"Came in through there," he remarked, with some satisfaction at the admiring silence of his audience of butler and footman. "There'd be a lot of dust outside on that sill, wouldn't there? And look at 'is trousers."

The audience bent its awed eyes on Major Bellingford Smart's nether garments, and the Major also looked down. Clearly marked on each knee was a circular patch of sooty grime which had certainly not been there before the Saint cannoned into him in that very helpful darkness.

On the far side of the square, Simon Templar heard the constable's whistle shrilling into the night, and drifted on towards the beer that waited for him.

THE NEW SWINDLE

Mr. Alfred Tillson ("Broads" Tillson to the trade) was only one of many men who cherished the hope that one day they might be privileged to meet the Saint again. Usually those ambitions included a dark night, a canal, and a length of lead pipe, with various trimmings and decorations according to the whim of the man concerned. But no bliss so unalloyed as that had ever come the way of any of those men; for canals and lengths of lead pipe did not enter into Simon Templar's own plans for his brilliant future, and on dark nights he walked warily as a matter of habit.

Mr. Alfred Tillson, however, enjoyed the distinction of being a man who did achieve his ambition and meet the Saint for a second time; although the recounter did not by any means take place as he would have planned it.

He was a lean, grey-haired man with a long, horse-like face and the air of a retired church-warden—an atmosphere which he had created for himself deliberately as an aid to business, and which he had practised for so long that in the end he could not have shaken it off if he had tried. It had become just as much a part of his natural make-up as the faintly ecclesiastical style of dress which he affected; and over the course of years it had served him well. For Mr. "Broads" Tillson, as his name conveyed, was acknowledged in the trade to be one of the greatest living card manipulators in the world. To see those long tapering fingers of his ruffling through a pack of cards and dealing out hands in which every pip had been considered and placed individually was an education in itself. He could do anything with a pack of cards except make it talk. He could shuffle it once, apparently without looking at it, and in that shuffle sort it out suit by suit and card by card, stack up any sequence he wanted, and put it all together again, with one careless flick of his hands that was too quick for the eye to follow. If you were in the trade, if you were "regular" and you could induce him to give you a demonstration of his magic, he would invite you to deal out four hands of bridge, write down a list of the cards in every hand, shuffle the pack again as much as you cared to, and give it back to him; whereupon he would take on glance at your list, shuffle the pack once himself, and proceed to deal out the four hands again exactly as you had listed them. And if you were unlucky enough to be playing with him in the way of business, you could order brand-new packs as often as you cared to pay for them, without inconveniencing him in the least. Mr. Alfred Tillson had never marked a card in his life; and he could play any card game that had ever been invented with equal success.

On the stage he might have made a very comfortable income for himself, but his tastes had never led him that way. Mr. Tillson was partial to travel and sea air; and for many years he had voyaged the Atlantic and Pacific ocean routes, paying himself very satisfactory dividends on every trip, and invariably leaving his victims with the consoling thought that they had at least evaded the wiles of sharpers and lost their money to an honest man. He might have retired long ago, if he had not had a weakness for beguiling the times beween voyages with dissipations of a highly unclerical kind; and as a matter of fact it was to this weakness of his that he owed his first meeting with the Saint.

He had made a very profitable killing on a certain trip which he took to Madeira; but coming back overland from Lisbon a sylph-like blonde detained him too long in Paris, and he woke up one morning to find that he was a full twenty pounds short of his fare to New York. He set out for London with this pressing need of capital absorbing his mind; and it was merely his bad luck that the elegant young man whom he discovered lounging idly over the rail when the cross-Channel boat left Boulogne should have been christened Simon Templar.

Simon was not looking for trouble on that trip, but he was never averse to having his expenses paid; and when Mr. Tillson hinted that it was distressingly difficult to find any congenial way of passing the time on cross-Channel journeys, he knew what to expect. They played casino, and Simon won fifteen pounds in the first half-hour.

"A bit slow, don't you think?" observed the benevolent Mr. Tillson, as he shuffled the cards at this point and called for another brace of double whiskies. "Shall we double the stakes?"

This was what Simon had been waiting for—and that gift of waiting for the psychological moment was one which he always employed on such occasions. Fifteen pounds was a small fish in his net, but who was he to criticise what a beneficent Providence cast kindly into his lap?

"Certainly, brother," he murmured. "Treble 'em if you like. I'll be with you again in a sec—I've just got to see a man about a small borzoi."

He faded away towards a convenient place; and that was the last Mr. Tillson saw of him. It was one of Mr. Tillson's saddest experiences; and three years later it was still as fresh in his memory as it had been the day after it happened. "Happy" Fred Jorman, that most versatile of small-time confidence men, whose round face creased up into such innumerable wrinkles of joy when he smiled, heard that "Broads" Tillson was in London, called on him on that third anniversary, and had to listen to the tale. They had worked together on one coup several years ago, but since then their ways had lain apart.

"That reminds me of a beggar I met this spring," said Happy Fred, not to be outdone in ancedote— and the ecclesiastical-looking Mr. Tillson hoped that "beggar" was the word he used. "I met him in the Alexandria—he seemed interested in horses, and he looked so lovely and innocent. When I told him about the special job I'd got for Newmarket that afternoon—"

This was one of Happy Fred's favourite stories, and much telling of it had tended to standardise the wording.

There was a certain prelude of this kind of conversation and general reminiscence before Happy Fred broached the real reason for his call.

"Between ourselves, Broads, things aren't going

too well in my business. There's too many stories in the newspapers these days to tell the suckers how it's done. Things have got so bad that one or two of the boys have had to go on the legit just to keep themselves alive."

"The circumstances are somewhat similar with me, Fred," confessed Mr. Tillson regretfully. "The Atlantic liners are half empty, and those gentlemen who are travelling don't seem to have the same surplus of lucre for the purposes of—um—recreation as they used to."

Happy Fred nodded.

"Well, that's how it struck me, Broads," he said. "And what with one thing and another, I said to myself, 'Fred,' I said, 'the old tricks are played out, and you'd better admit it. Fred,' I said, 'you've got to keep up with the times or go under. And what's wanted these days,' I said to myself, 'is a New Swindle.'"

Mr. Tillson raised his episcopal eyebrows.

"And have you succeeded in devising this—um —novel system of remunerative equivocation?"

"I *have* invented a new swindle, if that's what you mean," said Happy Fred. "At least, it's new enough for me. And the beauty of it is that you don't have to do anything criminal—anyway, not that anyone's going to know about. It's all quite straight and above-board, and whatever happens you can't get pinched for trying it, if you're clever enough about the way you work it."

"Have you made any practical experiments with this new method?" inquired Mr. Tillson.

"I haven't," said Happy Fred lugubriously. "And the trouble is that I can't. Here am I carrying this wonderful idea about with me, and I can't use it. That's why I've come to you. What I need, Broads, is a partner who won't doublecross me, who's clever with his hands, and hasn't got any kind of police record. That's why I can't do it myself. The bloke who does this has got to be a respectable bloke that nobody can say anything against. And that's where you come in. I've been worrying about it for weeks, thinking of all the good money there is waiting for me to pick up, and wondering who I could find to come in with me that I could trust. And then just last night somebody told me that you were back; and I said to myself, 'Fred,' I said, 'Broads Tillson is the very man you want. He's the man who'll give you a square deal, and won't go and blow your idea about.' So I made up my mind to come and see you and see what you felt about it. I'm willing to give you my idea, Broads, and put up the capital—I've got a bit of money saved up—if you'll count me in fifty-fifty."

"What is this idea?" asked Mr. Tillson cautiously.

Happy Fred helped himself to another drink, swallowed half of it, and wiped his mouth on the back of his hand.

"It goes like this," he said, with the unconscious reverence of a poet introducing his latest brainchild to the world. "You go to one of the big jewellers, posing as a rich man who's got a little bit of stuff in Paris, see? That ought to be easy for you. You want to send this girl a lovely big diamond necklace or something, and you choose something out of his stock that you can get for about a thousand quid— that's as much as I can put up. This necklace has got to be sent by post, and so of course it's got to be insured. Now it's made into a parcel; and all this time you've got in your pocket another box about the same size, with pebbles in it to make it about the same weight. This is where the man who does it has got to be clever with his hands, like you are. As soon as the necklace has been packed in its box—"

Mr. Tillson sighed.

"There's nothing new about that," he protested. "You haven't got the money to reimburse this jeweller for his necklace, and therefore you desire the sealed package to be preserved in his safe until you post him the money and request him to send it to you. And when he tires of waiting for his instructions he opens the package and discovers that you have absconded with the necklace and left him the receptacle containing the pebbles. That's a very old one, Fred, don't you think?"

"Haven't got the money nothing!" said Happy Fred scornfully. "Of course you've got the money —I tell you I'm putting up a thousand quid for this job. No jeweller would be taken in with that old trick you're thinking of these days—he'd send for the police as soon as you suggested it. You pay cash for this bit of jewellery you buy, and it's all square and above-board. Now listen to what I've got to say."

Mr. Alfred Tillson listened, and was impressed. Happy Fred's variation on an old theme appeared to have many of the qualities that were claimed for it by its proud inventor; and although it did not exactly come within Mr. Tillson's self-chosen province, it was true that the recent falling-off in transatlantic travel had left him particularly receptive to ideas that opened up new possibilities of income.

The new swindle is a thing that every confidence man dreams of creating: it is the brain-wave that sweeps through the trade once in a generation, and produces a golden harvest for its pioneers before the officious publicity of the press sends the soaring market slumping back again. Life is like that for *chevaliers d'industrie* like Happy Fred Jorman: the criminological trend of the Sunday newspapers reduces the ranks of the suckers every Sabbath, and the movies they see during the week haven't helped either. But this new swindle looked as if it might enjoy a fair run of success before it went the way of all other brilliant inventions.

Possibly it was because both partners in the new alliance were so pleased with the potentialities of their own brilliance that they temporarily forgot their common ambition to meet Simon Templar again—with a convenient canal and a length of lead pipe thrown in.

Simon himself was not thinking about them, for he had his own views on the kind of acquaintance which he was anxious to renew. Ruth Eden was a very different proposition. The fact that he had been privileged to rescue her in romantic circumstances from the attentions of the unspeakable Mr. Julian Lamantia, and that subsequently Mr. Lamantia had been one of three men who found themselves unexpectedly poorer for that meeting, included her among the register of people whom Simon Templar would have been pleased to meet again at any time. He had managed to get her a job with another acquaintance of his, who was such an exclusive jeweller that he had an office instead of a shop, and produced his treasures out of a vast safe instead of leaving them about in glass-topped counters; but after that he had heard nothing of her for some while.

She rang up one day about this time, and he was delighted to hear her voice. From the date of their first meeting she had exhibited commendable symptoms of hero-worship, and Simon Templar had no modesty in his composition.

"Have you forgotten me altogether?" she demanded; and the Saint chuckled into the transmitter.

"To tell you the truth, I've been so busy murdering people that I've hardly had a minute to spare. I thought you must have got married or something. Come and have dinner and see my collection of skulls."

"I'd love to. When?"

"Why not to-night? What time does Alan let you go?"

"Half-past five."

"I'll call for you at six—that'll just give you time to put your hat on, darling," said the Saint angelically, and rang off before she could make a suitable reply.

He was engaged in a running commentary on her inevitable feminine manoeuvres in front of a mirror in Alan Emberton's outer office, when the glass-panelled door of the inner sanctum opened, and the sound of a voice that seemed vaguely familiar made him break off short in the middle of a sentence. In another second, to her intense astonishment, he had vanished under a desk like a rabbit into its burrow; and if she had not turned abruptly back to her mirror while Emberton showed his client out she would have had to burst out laughing.

But Simon was on his feet again when the jeweller came back, and he was completely unruffled by his own extraordinary behaviour.

"Hullo, Templar," said Emberton, noticing him with some surprise. "Where did you spring from?"

He was a big man, with a jovial red face, who looked more like a retired butcher than an exclusive jeweller, and he liked the Saint in spite of his sins. He held out his beefy hand.

"I was under the desk," said the Saint unblushingly. "I dropped a penny and I was looking for it. How's life?"

"Not so good as it might be," answered the other frankly. "However, I suppose I can't grumble. I've just sold a thousand-pound diamond bracelet to that fellow I was showing out. Did you see him?"

"No," said the Saint untruthfully.

He had seen Mr. Alfred Tillson quite distinctly; and the problem of what Broads Tillson could possibly want with a thousand-pound diamond bracelet bothered him quite a lot in the taxi in which he carried Ruth Eden off to the West End. Broads Tillson, he knew, was often extravagantly generous to his lady friends; but somehow he could not associate thousand-pound bracelets even with that amorous man. Either Mr. Tillson had recently made no small click, or else there was more in that purchase than met the eye; and Simon had a constitutional objection to his old acquaintances embarking on enterprises of which he knew nothing.

The girl noticed his silence and challenged him.

"Why did you disappear under that desk, Simon? I feel there's some thrilling secret behind it."

"It was pure instinct," said the Saint brazenly, "to avoid being recognised. You see, Alan's latest client is one of the slickest cardsharpers in the world, and I once didled him out of fifteen quid that he threw out for ground-bait.''

Her eyes opened wide.

"Are you sure? Gee, why ever didn't you tell Mr. Emberton at once?"

"Because I'd like to know what his new trick is first." The blithe cavalier's blue eyes glinted at her mockingly. "Didn't you once tell me you'd love to be an adventurer's partner, Ruth? Well, here's a chance for you. Find out the whole details of the deal, every single fact you can get hold of, without saying anything to Alan. Give your best imitation of an adventuress worming out secrets so that the victim doesn't even know they've been wormed. And come and tell me. I'll promise you I'll see Alan doesn't get swindled; but wouldn't you hate to do anything so dull as just tell him to send for the police?"

She met him the next evening, full of excitement over the triumph of her maiden effort at sleuthing. She could hardly contain her news until he had ordered her a cocktail.

"I can't see the catch in it at all; but perhaps you can. Mr. Tillson gave Mr. Emberton a cheque for the bracelet yesterday, and he particularly asked Mr. Emberton to get a special clearance so that there wouldn't be any difficulty about it. So the cheque must be all right. Mr. Tillson is sending it to a friend of his in Paris for a birthday present, he says, and he's having it insured to go over. A valuer came from the insurance company to-day to have a look at it. Mr. Tillson—"

"Call him Broads," suggested the Saint. "He'd take it as a compliment."

"Why 'Broads'?" she asked, wrinkling her fore-head.

"'Broads' are cards, in the language. How exactly is this bracelet being sent?"

"By post. Mr. Till—Broads is coming in to-morrow to see it off and enclose a letter, and a man from the insurance company is coming down as well—that seems an awful lot of formality, but I suppose they have to be careful. Now what do you think will happen? Will Broads pull out a gun and hold us all up?"

"I doubt it," murmured the Saint mildly. "Broads isn't a violent man. Besides, if there was anything like that in the air he'd have done it yesterday. Let me think."

He leaned back and scowled thoughtfully into space. More than once he had truthfully admitted that the solving of ancient mysteries wasn't in his line; but the imaginative construction of forthcoming ones was another matter. The Saint's immoral mind worked best and most rapidly along those lines. . . . And then, as he scowled into space, a headline in the evening paper that was being read by a fat gent at an adjoining table percolated into his abstracted vision; and he sat up with a start that made the fat gent turn round and glare at him.

"I've got it!" he cried. "Whoops—and what a beauty!"

She caught at his sleeve.

"Tell me, Simon."

"No, darling. That I can't do—not till afterwards. But you shall hear it, if you like to meet me again on Saturday. What time is this posting party?"

"Eleven o'clock. But listen—I must tell Mr. Emberton—"

"You must do nothing of the sort." The Saint shook his head at her sadly. "What do you want to do, Ruth—ruin the only bit of business the poor man's done this week? He's got his money, hasn't he? The rest of the show is purely private."

When she continued to try and question him he returned idiotic answers that made her want to smack him; and she went home, provoked and disappointed, and not entirely consoled by his repeated promise to tell her the whole story after it was all over.

But her sense of excitement returned when Mr. Tillson presented himself at the office the next morning. Looking at that rather pathetically horse-faced gentleman in his faintly clerical garb, it was difficult to believe that he could possibly be the man that the Saint had described him. He was punctual to the minute; and the insurance company's representative came in soon afterwards. She showed them into the inner office, and found it easy to stay around herself while the package was being prepared and sealed. She watched the entire proceeding with what she would always believe was well-simulated unconcern, but which actually would have seemed like a hypnotic stare to anyone who had noticed her; and yet when it was all over and the various parties had shaken hands and departed, she could not recall the slightest incident that had deviated from the matter-of-fact formality which should have been expected of the affair. She even began to wonder, with a feeling that her doubt was almost sacrilegious, whether the Saint could have been mistaken. . . .

Mr. Alfred Tillson was not so reassured. He was perspiring a little when he met Happy Fred Jorman on the street corner.

"Yes, I effected the substitution," he said shortly, in answer to his partner's questions. "I trust I have aroused no suspicion. There was a kind of girl amanuensis in the room all the time, and she stared at me from the minute I arrived until the minute I left. I expected her to make some comment at any moment, but she took her eyes off me for a second when I knocked my hat off the desk. Let's get back to my hotel."

They took a taxi to the hotel in Bloomsbury where Mr. Tillson had taken a modest suite— Broads Tillson had luxurious tastes which had never helped him to save money, and he had insisted that this setting was necessary for the character he had to play. Happy Fred Jorman, whose liberty was not in jeopardy, was elated.

"That was just your imagination, Broads," he said as they let themselves in. "She was probably wishing she had a friend who sent her thousand-pound bracelets. It's just the newness of it that's upset you—you'll get used to it after you've done it a few times. I was saying to myself all the time you were practising, 'Fred,' I was saying, 'Broads Tillson rings the changes better than anyone else you've ever met in your life. You've picked the best partner—"

Mr. Tillson poured himself out a whisky-and-soda and sank into a chair. From his breast pocket he drew a packet with one seal on it—it was the exact replica of the packet that had been posted to Paris, as it had appeared after the first seal had been placed on it in Mr. Emberton's office.

"You'll have to fence the article, Fred," said Mr. Tillson. "I've never had anything to do with these things."

"I'll fence it all right," said Happy Fred. "We'll get four hundred for it easily. And then what happens? That other little packet I registered at the same time blows off and sets the mail-bag on fire in the train, and when they've cleared up the mess they find your bracelet is missing. Then there's just another sensational mail-bag robbery for the newspapers, and everybody's wondering how it was done; while we just collect the insurance money. That's four hundred pounds profit for a couple of hours' work, and we can turn that over every week while it lasts." Happy Fred slapped his thigh. "Gosh, Broads, when I think of the money we're going to make out of that idea of mine—"

"You might live to make it," remarked a very pleasant voice behind them, "if you both sat quite still."

The two men did not sit quite still. They would have been superhuman stoics if they had. They spun round as if they had each been hit on the side of the jaw with a blackjack and they saw the Saint.

The door of Mr. Tillson's private bath-room had opened and closed while they were talking without them hearing it; and now it served as a neat white background for the lean and smiling man who was propping himself gracefully up against it. There was an automatic in his hand, and it turned from side to side in a lazy arc that gave each of them an opportunity to blink down its black, uncompromising barrel.

"Possibly I intrude," murmured the Saint, very pleasantly; "but that's just too bad."

On the faces of the two men were expressions of mingled astonishment, fear, indignation, horror, and simple wrath, which would have done credit to a pair of dyspeptic cows that had received an electric shock from a clump of succulent grass. And then Mr. Tillson's voice returned.

"Good God!" he squeaked. "It's the man I was telling you about—"

"The bloke *I* was telling *you* about!" ejaculated Happy Fred savagely. "The skunk who took thirty pounds of my money in the Alexandra, and then—"

The two men's heads revolved until they looked into each other's eyes and gazed into the souls beyond. And the Saint hitched himself off the door and came towards them.

"A very neat piece of work, if I may say so, Fred," he remarked. "Not so original as it might have been, perhaps, but new enough. It's very kind of you to have worked so hard for me."

"What are you going to do?" asked Mr. Tillson weakly.

Simon took the packet out of his hands.

"Relieve you of this encumbrance, brother. It's a very pretty bracelet, but I don't think you could wear it. People might think it was rather odd."

"I'll have the police on to you for this, you—"
Simon raised his eyebrows.

"The police? To tell them that I've stolen your bracelet? But I understood your bracelet was in the post, on its way to your little girl in Paris? Can I be mistaken, Alfred?"

Mr. Tillson swallowed painfully; and then Happy Fred jumped up.

"Damn the police!" he snarled. "I'll settle with

this bluffer. He wouldn't dare to shoot—"

"Oh, but you're quite wrong about that," said the Saint gently. "I shouldn't have any objection to shooting you if you asked for it. It's quite a long time since I last shot anyone, and I often feel afraid that if I abstain for too long I may get squeamish. Don't tempt me, Fred, because I'm feeling nervous enough already."

But the Saint's blue eyes were as steady as the gun in his hand, and it was Happy Fred's gaze that wavered.

"I shall have to tie you up while I make my getaway," said the Saint amiably, "so would you both mind turning round? You'll be able to undo yourselves quite quickly after I've gone."

"You wouldn't be a party to a low insurance swindle, would you?" protested Happy Fred aggrievedly, as the Saint looped coils of rope deftly round his wrists.

"I wouldn't be a party to any kind of swindle," said the Saint virtuously. "I'm an honest hold-up man, and your insurance policies have nothing to do with me."

He completed the roping of the two men, roughly gagged them with their own handkerchiefs, and retreated leisurely to the door. Neither of them made any attempt to wave him good-bye, which Simon felt was rather rude.

THE FIVE THOUSAND POUND KISS

It has been said that Simon Templar was a philanderer; but the criticism was not entirely just. A pretty face, or the turn of a slim ankle, appealed to him no more—and not a bit less—than they do to the next man. Perhaps he was more honest about it.

It is true that sometimes, in a particularly buccaneering mood, as he swung down a broad highway leading to infinite adventure, he would sing one of his own inimitable songs against the pompous dreariness of civilisation as he saw it, with a chorus:

> *But if red blood runs thin with years,*
> *By God! if I must die,*
> *I'll kiss red lips and drink red wine*
> *And let the rest go by,*
> *My son,*
> *And let the rest go by!*

But there was a gesture in that, to be taken with or without salt as the audience pleased; and a fat lot the Saint cared. He was moderate in nothing that he said or did. That insurgent vitality which made him an outlaw first and last in everything rebelled perhaps too fiercely against all moderation; and if at the same time it made him, to those who knew him best, the one glamorous and romantic figure of his day, that was the judgment which he himself would have asked for.

These chronicles are concerned mainly with episodes in which he provided himself with the bare necessities of life by cunning and strategy rather than daring; but even in those times there were occasions when his career hung on the thread of a lightning decision. That happened in the affair of Mrs. Dempster-Craven's much-advertised pink diamond; and if the Saint philandered then, he would have told you that he had no regrets.

"The idea that such a woman should have a live jewel like that keeps me awake at nights," he complained. "I've seen her twice, and she is a Hag."

This was at dinner one night. Peter Quentin was there; and so was Patricia Holm, who, when all was said and done, was the lady who held the Saint's reckless heart and knew best how to understand all his misdeeds. The subject of the "Star of Mandalay" had cropped up casually in the course of conversation; and it is worth mentioning that neither of Simon Templar's guests bothered to raise any philosophical argument agains his somewhat heterodox doctrine about the rights of Hags. But it was left for Peter Quentin to put his foot in it.

Peter read behind the wistfulness of the Saint's words, and said: "Don't be an idiot, Simon. You don't need the money, and you couldn't pinch the

Star of Mandalay. The woman's got a private detective following her around wherever she goes—"

"Couldn't I pinch it, Peter?" said the Saint, very softly.

Patricia saw the light in his eyes, and clutched Peter's wrist.

"You ass!" she gasped. "Now you've done it. He'd be fool enough to try—"

"Why 'try'?" asked the Saint, looking round mildly. "That sounds very much like an aspersion on my genius, which I shall naturally have to—"

"I didn't mean it like that," protested the girl frantically. "I mean that after all, when we don't need the money—You said you were thinking of running over to Paris for a week—"

"We can go via Amsterdam, and sell the Star of Mandalay *en route,*" said the Saint calmly. "You lie in your teeth, my sweetheart. You meant that the Star of Mandalay was too much of a problem for me and I'd only get in a mess if I tried for it. Well, as a matter of fact, I've been thinking of having a dart at it for some time."

Peter Quentin drank deeply of the Chambertin to steady his nerves.

"You haven't been thinking anything of the sort," he said. "I'll withdraw everything I said. You were just taking on a dare."

Simon ordered himself a second slice of melon, and leaned back with his most seraphic and exasperating smile.

"Have I," he inquired blandly, "ever told you my celebrated story about a bob-tailed ptarmigan named Alphonse, who lived in sin with a couple of duck-billed platypi in the tundras of Siberia? Alphonse, who suffered from asthma and was a believer in Christian Science. . . ."

He completed his narrative at great length, refusing to be interrupted; and they knew that the die was cast. When once Simon Templar had made up his mind it was impossible to argue with him. If he didn't proceed blandly to talk you down with one of his most fatuous and irrelevant anecdotes, he would listen politely to everything you had to say, agree with you thoroughly, and carry on exactly as he had announced his intentions from the beginning; which wasn't helpful. And he had made up his mind, on one of his mad impulses, that the Star of Mandalay was due for a change of ownership. It was not a very large stone, but it was reputed to be flawless; and it was valued at ten thousand pounds. Simon reckoned that it would be worth five thousand pounds to him in Van Roeper's little shop in Amsterdam, and five thousand pounds was a sum of money that he could find a home for at any time.

But he said nothing about that to Mrs. Dempster-Craven when he saw her for the third time and spoke to her for the first. He was extremely polite and apologetic. He had good reason to be, for the rakish Hirondel which he was driving had collided with Mrs. Dempster-Craven's Rolls Royce in Hyde Park, and the glossy symmetry of the Rolls Royce's rear elevation had been considerably impaired.

"I'm terribly sorry," he said. "Your chauffeur pulled up rather suddenly, and my hand-brake cable broke when I tried to stop."

His hand-brake cable had certainly divided itself in the middle, and the frayed ends had been produced for the chauffeur's inspection; but no one was to know that Simon had filed it through before he started out.

"That is not my fault," said Mrs. Dempster-Craven coldly. She was going to pay a call on the wife of a minor baronet, and she was pardonably annoyed at the damage to her impressive car. "Bagshawe, will you please find me a taxi."

"The car'll take you there all right, ma'am," said the chauffeur incautiously.

Mrs. Dempster-Craven froze him through her lorgnettes.

"How," she required to know, "can I possibly call on Lady Wiltham in a car that looks as if I had picked it up at a second-hand sale? Kindly call me a taxi immediately, and don't argue."

"Yes, ma'am," said the abashed chauffeur, and departed on his errand.

"I really don't know how to apologise," said the Saint humbly.

"Then don't try," said Mrs. Dempster-Craven discouragingly.

The inevitable small crowd had collected, and a policeman was advancing ponderously towards it from the distance. Mrs. Dempster-Craven liked to be stared at as she crossed the pavement to Drury Lane Theatre on a first night, but not when she was sitting in a battered car in Hyde Park. But the Saint was not so self-conscious.

"I'm afraid I can't offer you a lift at the moment; but if my other car would be of any use to you for the reception to-night—"

"What reception?" asked Mrs. Dempster-Craven haughtily, having overcome the temptation to retort that she had three other Rolls Royces no less magnificent than the one she was sitting in.

"Prince Marco d'Ombria's," answered the Saint easily. "I heard you say that you were going to call on Lady Wiltham, and I had an idea that I'd heard Marco mention her name. I thought perhaps—"

"I am not going to the reception," said Mrs. Dempster-Craven; but it was noticeable that her tone was not quite so freezing. "I have a previous engagement to dine with Lord and Lady Bredon."

Simon chalked up the point without batting an eyelid. He had not engineered that encounter without making inquiries about his victim, and it had not taken him long to learn that Mrs. Dempster-Craven's one ambition was to win for herself and her last husband's millions an acknowledged position among the Very Best People. That carelessly dropped reference to a Prince, even an Italian Prince, by his first name, had gone over like a truck-load of honey. And it was a notable fact that if Mrs. Dempster-Craven had pursued her own inquiries into the reference, she would have found that the name of Simon Templar was not only recognised but hailed effusively; for there had once been a spot of bother involving a full million pounds belonging to the Bank of Italy which had made the Saint for ever *persona grata* at the Legation.*

The chauffeur returned with a taxi, and Mrs. Dempster-Craven's fifteen stones of flesh were assisted ceremoniously out of the Rolls. Having had a brief interval to consider pros and cons, she deigned to thank the Saint for his share in the oper-

*See *The Saint vs. Scotland Yard*.

ation with a smile that disclosed a superb set of expensive teeth.

"I hope your car isn't seriously damaged," she remarked graciously; and the Saint smiled in his most elegant manner.

"It doesn't matter a bit. I was just buzzing down to Hurlingham for a spot of tennis, but I can easily take a taxi." He took out his wallet and handed her a card. "As soon as you know what the damage'll cost to put right, I do hope you'll send me in the bill."

"I shouldn't dream of doing such a thing," said Mrs. Dempster-Craven. "The whole thing was undoubtedly Bagshawe's fault."

With which startling *volte-face,* and another display of her expensive denture, she ascended regally into the cab; and Simon Templar went triumphantly back to Patricia.

"It went off perfectly, Pat! You could see the whole line sizzling down her throat till she choked on the rod. The damage to the Hirondel will cost about fifteen quid to put right, but we'll charge that up to expenses. And the rest of it's only a matter of time."

The time was even shorter than he had expected; for Mrs. Dempster-Craven was not prepared to wait any longer than was necessary to see her social ambitions fulfilled, and the highest peak she had attained at that date was a week-end at the house of a younger son of a second viscount.

Three days later Simon's postbag included a scented mauve envelope, and he knew before he opened it that it was the one he had been waiting for.

* * *

118, *Berkeley Square,*
Mayfair, W.I.

My dear Mr. Templar,

I'm sure you must have thought me rather abrupt after our accident in Hyde Park on Tuesday, but these little upsets seem so much worse at the time than they really are. Do try to forgive my rudeness.

I am having a little party here on Thursday next. Lord and Lady Palfrey are coming, and the Hon. Celia Mallard, and lots of other people whom I expect you'll know. I'd take it as a great favour if you could manage to look in, any time after 9.30, just to let me know you weren't offended.

I do hope you got to Hurlingham all right.

Yours sincerely,
Gertrude Dempster-Craven.

"Who said my technique had ever failed me?" Simon demanded of Peter Quentin at lunch-time that day.

"I didn't," said Peter, "as I've told you all along. Thank God you won't be going to prison on Thursday, anyway—if it's only a little party she's invited you to. I don't suppose you'll even see the Star of Mandalay."

Simon grinned.

"Little party be blowed," he said. "Gertrude has never thrown a little party in her life. When she talks about a 'little' party she means there'll only be two orchestras and not more than a hundred couples. And if she doesn't put on the Star of Mandalay for Lady Palfrey's benefit I am a bobtailed ptarmigan and my name is Alphonse."

Nevertheless, when he suggested that Peter

Quentin should come with him there was not much argument.

"How can you get me in?" Peter demurred. "I wasn't invited, and I don't know any princes."

"You've got an uncle who's a lord or something, haven't you?"

"I've got an uncle who's the Bishop of Johannesburg; but what does Mrs. Dempster-Craven care about South African bishops?"

"Call him Lord Johannesburg," said the Saint. "She won't look him up in Debrett while you're there. I'll say we were dining together and I couldn't shake you off."

At that point it all looked almost tediously straightforward, a commonplace exploit with nothing but the size of the prize to make it memorable. And when Simon arrived in Berkeley Square on the date of his invitation it seemed easier still; for Mrs. Dempster-Craven, as he had expected, was proudly sporting the Star of Mandalay on her swelling bosom, set in the centre of a pattern of square-cut sapphires in a platinum pendant that looked more like an illuminated sky-sign than anything else. True, there was a large-footed man in badly fitting dress clothes who trailed her around like a devoted dachshund; but private detectives of any grade the Saint felt competent to deal with. Professionals likewise, given a fair warning—although he was anticipating no professional surveillance that night. But he had not been in the house twenty minutes before he found himself confronting a dark, slender girl with merry brown eyes whose face appeared before him like the Nemesis of one of his most innocent flirtations—and even then he did not guess what

Fate had in store for him.

At his side he heard the voice of Mrs. Dempster-Craven cooing like a contralto dove:

"This is Miss Rosamund Armitage—a cousin of the Duke of Trayall." And then, as she saw their eyes fixed on each other: "But have you met before?"

"Yes—we have met," said the Saint, recovering himself easily. "Wasn't it that day when you were just off to Ostend?"

"I think so," said the girl gravely.

A plaintive baronet in search of an introduction accosted Mrs. Dempster-Craven from the other side, and Simon took the girl in his arms as the second orchestra muted its saxophones for a waltz.

"This is a very happy reunion, Kate," he murmured. "I must congratulate you."

"Why?" she asked suspiciously.

"When we last met—in that famous little argument about the Kellman necklace—you weren't so closely related to the Duke of Trayall."

They made a circuit of the floor—she danced perfectly, as he would have expected—and then she said, bluntly: "What are you doing here, Saint?"

"Treading the light fantastic—drinking free champagne—and watching little monkeys scrambling up the social ladder," he answered airily. "And you?"

"I'm here for exactly the same reason as you are —my old-age pension."

"I can't imagine you getting old, Kate."

"Let's sit out somewhere," she said suddenly.

They left the ballroom and went in search of a secluded corner of the conservatory, where there were arm-chairs and sheltering palm trees providing discreet alcoves for romantic couples. Simon noticed that the girl was quite sure of her way around, and said so.

"Of course I've been here before," she said. "I expect you have, too."

"On the contrary—this is my first visit. I never take two bites at a cherry."

"Not even a ten thousand pound one?"

"Not even that."

She produced a packet of cigarettes from her bag and offered him one. Simon smiled, and shook his head.

"There are funny things about your cigarettes that don't make me laugh out loud, Kate," he said cheerfully. "Have one of mine instead."

"Look here," she said. "Let's put our cards on the table. You're after that pendant, and so am I. Everything on our side is planned out, and you've just told me this is your first visit. You can't possibly get in front of us this time. You took the Kellman necklace away under our noses, but you couldn't do it again. Why not retire gracefully?"

He gazed at her thoughtfully for a few seconds; and she touched his hand.

"Won't you do that—and save trouble?"

"You know, Kate," said the Saint, "you're a lovely child. Would you mind very much if I kissed you?"

"I could make it worth a hundred pounds to you —for nothing—if you gave us a clear field."

Simon wrinkled his nose.

"Are there forty-nine of you?" he drawled. "It seems a very small share-out to me."

"I might be able to make it two hundred. They wouldn't agree to any more."

The Saint blew smoke-rings towards the ceiling.

"If you could make it two thousand I don't think you'd be able to buy me off, darling. Being bought off is so dull. So what's the alternative? Am I slugged with another sandbag and locked up in the pantry?"

Suddenly he found that she was gripping his arm, looking straight into his face.

"I'm not thinking about your health, Saint," she said quietly. "I want that pendant. I want it more than I'd expect you to believe. I've never asked any other man a favour in my life. I know that in our racket men don't do women favours—without getting paid for it. But you're supposed to be different, aren't you?"

"This is a new act, Kate," murmured the Saint interestedly. "Do go on—I want to hear what the climax is."

"Do you think this is an act?"

"I don't want to be actually rude, darling, especially after all the dramatic fervour you put into it, but—"

"You've got every right to think so," she said; and he saw that the merriment was gone from her great brown eyes. "I should think the same way if I were in your place. I'll try to keep the dramatic fervour out of it. Can I tell you—that that pendant means the way out of the racket for me? I'm going straight after this." She was twisting her handkerchief, turning away from him now. "I'm going to get married—on the level. Funny, isn't it?"

He glanced at her doubtfully, with that mocking curve still lingering on his lips. For some reason he refrained from asking whether her other husbands had been informed of this plan: he knew nothing about her private life. But even with the best intentions a modern Robin Hood must get that way; and he did not know why he was silent.

And then, quite clearly, he heard the tread of leisurely feet on the other side of the clump of imported vegetation behind which they were concealed. Instinctively they glanced at one another, listening, and heard a man's fat chuckle beyond the palms.

"I guess that new plan makes it a lot easier than the way we were going to work it."

Simon saw the girl half rising from the settee. In a flash he had flung one arm round her, pinning her down, and clapped his other hand over her mouth.

"Maybe it'll save a little trouble, anyway," spoke the second man. There came the scratch of a match, and then: "What are you doing about the girl?"

"I don't know. . . . She's a pretty little piece, but she's getting too serious. I'll have to ditch her in Paris."

"She'll be sore."

"Well, she ought to know how to take the breaks. I had to keep her going to get us in here, but it ain't my fault if she wants to make it a permanency."

"What about her share?"

"Aw, I might send her a coupla hundred, just for conscience money. She ain't a bad kid. Too sentimental, that's all."

A short pause, and then the second man again:

"Well, that's your business. It's just a quarter after eleven. Guess I better see Watkins and make sure he's ready to fix those lights."

The leisured feet receded again; and Simon released the girl slowly. He saw that she was as white as a sheet, and there were strange tears in her eyes. He lighted a cigarette methodically. It was a tough life for women—always had been. They had to know how to take the breaks.

"Did you hear?" she asked, and he looked at her again.

"I couldn't very well help it. I'm sorry, kid. . . . That was your prospective husband, I suppose?"

She nodded.

"Anyway, you'll know it wasn't an act."

There was nothing he could say. She stood up, and he walked beside her back to the ball-room. She left him there, with a smile that never trembled; and the Saint turned and found Peter Quentin beside him.

"Must you keep all the fun to yourself, old boy?" pleaded Peter forlornly. "I've been treading on the toes of the fattest dowager in the world. Who's your girl friend? She looks a stunner."

"She stunned me once," said the Saint reminiscently. "Or some pals of hers did. She's passing here as Rosamund Armitage; but the police know her best as Kate Allfield, and her nickname is The Mug."

Peter's eyes were following the girl yearningly across the room.

"There ought to be some hideous punishment for bestowing names like that," he declared; and the Saint grinned absent-mindedly.

"I know. In a story-book she'd be Isabelle de la Fontaine; but her parents weren't thinking about her career when they christened her. That's real life in our low profession—and so is the nickname."

"Does that mean there's competition in the field?"

"It means just that." Simon's gaze was sweeping systematically over the other guests; and at that moment he saw the men he was looking for. "You see that dark bird who looks as if he might be a gigolo? Face like a pretty boy, till you see it's just a mask cut in granite. . . . That's Philip Carney. And the big fellow beside him—just offering the Dempster-Craven a cigarette. That's George Runce. They're two of the slickest jewel thieves in the business. Mostly they work the Riviera—I don't think they've ever been in England before. Kate was talking in the plural all the time, and I wondered who she meant."

Peter's mouth shaped a silent whistle.

"What's going to happen?"

"I don't know definitely; but I should like to prophesy that at any moment the lights will go out—"

And as he spoke, with a promptness that seemed almost uncanny, the three enormous cut-glass chandeliers which illuminated the ball-room simultaneously flicked out as if a magic wand had conjured them out of existence; and the room was plunged into inky blackness.

The buzz of conversation rose louder, mingled with sporadic laughter. After trying valiantly to carry on for a couple of bars, the orchestra faded out irregularly, and the dancers shuffled to a standstill. Over in one corner, a facetious party started singing, in unison: "Where—was—Moses—when —the—lights—went—out?" . . . And then, rising above every other sound, came Mrs. Dempster-Craven's hysterical shriek:

"Help!"

There was a momentary silence, broken by a few uncertain titters. And Mrs. Dempster-Craven's voice rang wildly through the room again.

"My pendant! My pendant! Put on the lights!"

Then came the sharp, vicious smash of a fist against flesh and bone, a coughing grunt, and the thud of a fall. Peter Quentin felt around him, but the Saint was gone. He started across the room, plunging blindly among the crowd that was heaving helplessly in the darkness. Then one or two matches flared up, and the light grew as other matches and lighters were struck to augment the illumination. And just as suddenly as they had gone out, the great chanceliers lighted up again.

Peter Quentin looked at the scene from the front rank of the circle of guests. George Runce was lying on the floor, with blood trickling from a cut in his chin; and a couple of yards from him sat Simon Templar, holding his jaw tenderly. Between them lay Mrs. Dempster-Craven's priceless pendant, with the chain broken; and while Peter looked she snatched it up with a sob, and he saw that the Star of Mandalay was missing from its centre.

"My diamond!" she wailed. "It's gone!"

Her private detective came elbowing through the back of the crowd, pushing Peter aside, and grabbed the Saint's shoulder.

"Come on, you!" he barked. "What happened?"

"There's your man," said the Saint, pointing to the unconscious figure beside him. "As soon as the lights went out, he grabbed the pendant—"

"That's a lie!"

Philip Carney had fallen on his knees beside Runce, and was loosening the man's collar. He turned round and yapped the denial indignantly enough; but Peter saw that his face had gone pale.

"I was standing beside Mr. Runce." He pointed to the Saint. "That man snatched the pendant, and Mr. Runce tried to stop him getting away."

"Why weren't you here, Watkins?" wailed Mrs. Dempster-Craven, shaking the detective wildly by the arm. "Why weren't you watching? I shall never see my diamond again—"

"I'm sorry, madam," said the detective—"I just left the room for one minute to find a glass of water. But I think we've got the man all right." He bent down and hauled the Saint to his feet. "We'd better search this fellow, and one of the footmen can go for the police while we're doing it."

Peter saw that the Saint's face had gone hard as polished teak. In Simon's right hand was the Star of Mandalay, pressed against his jaw as he was holding it. As soon as the lights had gone out he had guessed what was going to happen: he had crossed the floor like a cat, grasped it neatly as Runce tore it out of its setting, and sent the big man flying with one well-directed left. All that he had been prepared for; but there were wheels turning that he had never reckoned with.

He looked the detective in the eyes.

"The less you talk about the police the better," he said quietly. "I was in the conservatory a few minutes ago, and I happened to hear Mr. Carney say: 'I'd better see Watkins and make sure he's ready to fix those lights.' I didn't think anything of it at the time, but this looks like an explanation."

There was an instant's deadly silence; and then Philip Carney laughed.

"That's one of the cleverest tricks I've ever heard

of," he remarked. "But it's a bit libellous, isn't it?"

"Not very," said a girl's clear voice.

Again the murmur of talk was stifled as if a blanket had been dropped on it; and in the hush Kate Allfield came into the front of the crowd. George Runce was rising on his elbows, and his jaw dropped as he heard her voice. She gave him one contemptuous glance, and faced Mrs. Dempster-Craven with her head erect.

"It's perfectly true," she said. "I was with Mr. Templar in the conservatory, and I heard it as well."

Carney's face had gone grey.

"The girl's raving," he said; but his voice was a little shaky. "I haven't been in the conservatory this evening."

"Neither have I," said Runce, wiping the frozen incredulity off his features with an effort. "I'll tell you what it is—"

But he did not tell them what it was; for at that point a fresh authoritative voice interrupted the debate with a curt "Make way, please," and the crowd opened to let through the burly figure of a detective-sergeant in plain clothes. Simon looked round, and saw that he had posted a constable at the door as he came in. The sergeant scanned the faces of the group, and addressed Mrs. Dempster-Craven.

"What's the trouble, madam?"

"My pendant—"

She was helped out by a chorus of bystanders whose information, taken in the mass, was somewhat confusing. The sergeant sorted it out phlegmatically; and at the end he shrugged.

"Since these genlemen are all accusing each other, I take it you don't wish to make any particular charges?"

"I cannot accuse my guests of being thieves," said Mrs. Dempster-Craven imperially. "I only want my diamond."

The sergeant nodded. He had spent twelve years in C Division, and had learned that Berkeley Square is a region where even policemen have to be tactful.

"In that case," he said, "I think it would help us if the gentlemen agreed to be searched."

The Saint straightened up.

It had been a good evening; and he had no regrets. The game was worth playing for its own sake, to him: the prizes came welcomely, but they weren't everything. And no one knew better than he that you couldn't win all the time. There were chances that couldn't be reckoned with in advance; and the duplicity of Mr. Watkins was one of those. But for that, he would have played his hand faultlessly, out-bluffed and out-manoeuvred the Carney-Runce combination in a fair field, and made as clean a job of it as anything else he had done. But that single unexpected factor had turned the scale just enough to bring the bluff to a showdown, as unexpected factors always would. And yet Peter Quentin saw that the Saint was smiling.

"I think that's a good idea," said the Saint.

Between Philip Carney and George Runce flashed one blank glance; but their mouths remained closed.

"Perhaps there's another room we could go to," said the sergeant, almost genially; and Mrs. Dempster-Craven inclined her head like a queen dismissing a distasteful odour.

"Watkins will show you to the library."

Simon turned on his heel and led the way towards the door, with Mr. Watkins still gripping his arm; but as his path brought him level with Kate Allfield he stopped and smiled down at her.

"I think you're a swell kid," he said.

His voice sounded a trifle strange. And then, before two hundred shocked and startled eyes, including those of Lord and Lady Bredon, the Honourable Celia Mallard, three baronets, and the aspiring Mrs. Dempster-Craven herself, he laid his hands gently on her shoulders and kissed her outrageously on the mouth; and in the silence of appalled aristocracy which followed that performance made his stately exit.

"How the devil did you get away with it?" asked Peter Quentin weakly, as they drove away in a taxi an hour later. "I was fairly sweating blood all the time you were being stripped."

The Saint's face showed up in the dull glow as he drew on his cigarette.

"It was in my mouth," he said.

"But they made you open your mouth—"

"It was there when I kissed Kate, anyway," said the Saint, and sang to himself all the rest of the way home.

THE BLIND SPOT

It is rather trite to remark that the greatest and sublimest of characters always have concealed in them somewhere a speck of human jelly that wobbles furtively behind the imposing armour-plate, as if Nature's sense of proportion refused to tolerate such a thing as a perfect superman. Achilles had his heel. The hard-boiled hoodlum of the Volstead Act weeps openly to the strains of a syncopated Mammy song. The learned judge gravely inquires: "What is a gooseberry?" The Cabinet Minister prances pontifically about the badminton court. The professor of theology knows the Saint Saga as well as the Epistle to the Ephesians. These things are familiar to every student of the popular newspapers.

But to Simon Templar they were more than mere curious facts, to be ranked with "Believe-it-or-not" strips of cigarette cards describing the architectural principles of the igloo. They were the very practical psychology of his profession.

"Every man on earth has at least one blind spot somewhere," Simon used to say, "and once you've found that spot you've got him. There's always some simple little thing that'll undermine his resistance, or some simple little trick that he's never heard of. A high-class cardsharper might never persuade him to play bridge for more than a half-penny a hundred, and yet a three-card man at Brooklands might take a fiver off him in five minutes. Develop that into a complete technique, and you can live in luxury without running any risks of getting brain fever."

One of Simon Templar's minor weaknesses was an insatiable curiosity. He met Patricia at Charing Cross underground station one afternoon with a small brown bottle.

"A man at the Irving Statue sold me this for a shilling," he said.

The broad reach of pavement around the Irving Statue, at the junction of Green Street and Charing Cross Road, is one of the greatest open-air theatres in London. Every day, at lunch-time, idle crowds gather there in circles around the performers on the day's bill, who carry on their work simultaneously like a three-ring circus. There is the Anti-Socialist tub-thumper, the numerologist, the strong man, the Negro selling outfits to enable you to do the three-card trick in your own home, the handcuff escape king, the patent medicine salesman, every kind of huckster and street showman takes up his pitch there on one day or another and holds his audience spellbound until the time comes for passing round the hat. Simon rarely passed there without pausing to inspect the day's offerings, but this was the first occasion on which he had been a buyer.

His bottle appeared to contain a colourless fluid like water, with a slight sediment of brownish particles.

"What is it?" asked Patricia.

"Chromium plating for the home," he said. "The greatest invention of the century—according to the salesman. Claimed to be the same outfit sold by mail-order firms for three bob. He was demonstrating it on a brass shell-case and on old Primus and brass door-knobs and what not, and it looked swell. Here, I'll show you."

He fished a penny out of his pocket, uncorked the bottle, and poured a drop of the liquid on to the coin. The tarnished copper cleared and silvered itself under her eyes, and when he rubbed it with his handkerchief it took a silvery polish like stainless steel.

"Boy, that's marevellous!" breathed Patricia dreamily. "You know that military sort of coat of mine, the one with the brass buttons? We were wanting to get them chromiumed—"

The Saint sighed.

"And that," he said, "is approximately what the cave woman thought of first when her battle-scarred Man dragged home a vanquished leopard. My darling, when will you realise that we are first and foremost a business organisation?"

But at that moment he had no clear idea of the profitable purposes to which his purchase might be put. The Saint had an instinct and a collecting passion for facts and gadgets that "might come in useful," but at the times when he acquired them he could rarely have told you what use they were ever likely to be.

He corked the bottle and put it away in his pocket. The train they were waiting for was signalled, and the rumble of its approach could be felt underfoot. Down in the blackness of the tunnel its lights swept round a bend and drove towards the platform; and it was quite by chance that the Saint's wandering glance flickered over the shabbily dressed elderly man who waited a yard away on his left, and fixed on him with a sudden razor-edged intentness that was more intuitive than logical. Or perhaps the elderly man's agitation was too transparent to be ordinary, his eyes too strained and haggard to be reassuring. . . . Simon didn't know.

The leading draught of the train fanned on his face; and then the elderly man clenched his fist and jumped. A woman screamed. "You blithering idiot!" snapped the Saint, and jumped also.

His feet touched down neatly inside the track. By some brilliant fluke the shabby man's blind leap had missed the live rail, and he was simply cowering where he had landed with one arm covering his eyes. The train was hardly more than a yard away when the Saint picked him up and heaved him back on to the platform, flinging himself off the line in the opposite direction as he did so. The train whisked by so close to him that it brushed his sleeve, and squeaked to a standstill with hissing brakes.

The Saint slid back the nearest door on his side, swung himself up from the track, and stepped through the coach to the platform. A small crowd had gathered round the object of his somewhat sensational rescue, and Simon shouldered a path through them unceremoniously. He knew that one of the many sublimely intelligent laws of England ordains that any person who attempts to take his own life shall, if he survives, be prosecuted and at the discretion of the Law imprisoned, in order that he may be helped to see that life is after all a very jolly business and thoroughly worth living; and such a flagrant case as the one Simon had just witnessed seemed to call for some distinctly prompt initiative.

"How d'you feel, old chap?" asked the Saint, dropping on one knee beside the man.

"I saw him do it," babbled a fat woman smugly. "With my own eyes I saw it. Jumped in front of the train as deliberate as you please. I saw him."

"I'm afraid you're mistaken, madam," said the Saint quietly. "This gentleman is a friend of mine. He's subject to rather bad fits, and one of them must have taken him just as the train was coming in. He was standing rather close to the edge of the platform, and he simply fell over."

"A very plucky effort of yours, sir, getting him out of the way," opined a white-whiskered retired colonel. "Very plucky, by Gad!"

Simon Templar, however, was not looking for bouquets. The shabby man was sitting motionless with his head in his hands: the desperation that had driven him into that spasmodic leap had left him, and he was trembling silently in a helpless reaction. Simon slipped an arm round him and lifted him to his feet; and as he did so the guard broke through the crowd.

"I shall 'ave to make a report of this business, sir," he said.

"Lord—I'm not going to be anybody's hero!" said the Saint. "My name's Abraham Lincoln, and this is my uncle, Mr. Christopher Columbus. You can take it or leave it."

"But if the gentleman's going to make any claim against the company I shall 'ave to make a report, sir," pleaded the guard plaintively.

"There'll be no complaints except for wasting time, Ebenezer," said the Saint. "Let's go."

He helped his unresisting salvage into a compartment, and the crowd broke up. The District Railway resumed its day's work; and Simon Templar lighted a cigarette and glanced whimsically at Patricia.

"What d'you think we've picked up this time, old dear?" he murmured.

The girl's hand touched his arm, and she smiled.

"When you went after him I was wondering what I'd lost," she said.

The Saint's quick smile answered her; and he returned to a scrutiny of his acquisition. The shabby man was recovering himself slowly, and Simon thought it best to leave him to himself for a while. By the time they had reached Mark Lane station he seemed to have become comparatively normal, and Simon stood up and jerked a thumb.

"C'mon, uncle. This is as far as I go."

The shabby man shook his head weakly.

"Really, I don't—"

"Step out," said the Saint.

The man obeyed listlessly; and Simon took his arm and piloted him towards the exit. They turned into a convenient café and found a deserted corner.

"I took a bit of trouble to pull you out of a mess, uncle, and the story of your life is the least you can give me in return."

"Are you a reporter?" asked the other wearily.

"I have a conscience," said the Saint. "What's your name, and what do you do?"

"Inwood. I'm a chemist and—a sort of inventor." The shabby man gazed apathetically at the cup of coffee which had been set before him. "I ought to thank you for saving my life, I suppose, but—"

"Take it as a gift," said the Saint breezily. "I was only thinking of our lines. I've got a few shares in the company, and your method of suicide makes such a mess. Now tell me why you did it."

Inwood looked up.

"Are you going to offer me charity?"

"I never do that. My charity begins at home, and stays on with Mother like a good girl."

"I suppose you've got some sort of right to an answer," said Inwood tiredly. "I'm a failure, that's all."

"And aren't we all?" said the Saint. "What did you fail at, uncle?"

"Inventing. I gave up a good job ten years ago to try and make a fortune on my own, and I've been living from hand to mouth ever since. My wife had a small income of her own, and I lived on that. I did one or two small things, but I didn't make much out of them. I suppose I'm not such a genius as I thought I was, but I believed in myself then. A month or so ago, when we were right at the end of our tether, I did make a little discovery."

The shabby man took from his pocket a small brass tube like a girl's lipstick case, and tossed it across the table. Simon removed the cap, and saw something like a crayon—it was white outside, with a pink core.

"Write something—with your pen, I mean," said Inwood.

Simon took out his fountain pen and scribbled a couple of words on the back of the menu. Inwood blew on it till it dried, and handed it back.

"Now rub it over with that crayon."

Simon did so, and the writing disappeared. It vanished quite smoothly and easily, at a couple of touches, without any hard rubbing, and the paper was left without a trace of discoloration or roughness.

"Just a useful thing for banks and offices," said Inwood. "There's nothing else like it. An ink eraser tears up the paper. You can buy a chemical bleacher, and several firms use it, but that's liquid —two reagents in separate bottles, and you have to put on drops of first one and then the other. That thing of mine is twice as simple and three times quicker."

Simon nodded.

"You're not likely to make a million out of it, but it ought to have quite a reasonable sale."

"I know that," said Inwood bitterly. "I didn't want a million. I'd have been glad to get a thousand. I've told you—I'm not such a genius as I thought I was. But a thousand pounds would have put us on our feet again—given me a chance to open a little shop or find a steady job or something. But I'm not going to get a penny out of it. It isn't my property—and I invented it! . . . We've been living on capital as well as income. This would have put us straight. It had to be protected." The old man's faded eyes blinked at the Saint pitifully. "I don't know anything about things like that. I saw a patent agent's advertisement in a cheap paper, and took it to him. I gave him all my formulae —everything. That was a fortnight ago. He told me he'd have to make a search of the records before any patent could be taken out. I had a letter from him this morning, and he said that a similar specification had been filed three days ago."

The Saint said nothing; but his blue eyes were suddenly very clear and hard.

"You see what it was?" In his weakness the shabby inventor was almost sobbing. "He swindled me. He gave my specifications to a friend of his and let him file them in his own name. I couldn't believe it. I went to the Patent Office myself this morning: a fellow I found there helped me to find what I wanted. Every figure in the specification was mine. It *was* my specification. The coincidence couldn't possibly have been so exact, even if somebody else *had* been working on the same idea at the same time as I was. But I can't prove anything. I haven't a shilling to fight him with. D'you hear? He's ruined me—"

"Steady on, uncle," said the Saint gently. "Have you seen this bird again?"

"I'd just left his office when—when you saw me at Charing Cross," said Inwood shakily. "He threw me out. When he found he couldn't bluff me he didn't bother to deny anything. Told me to go on and prove it, and be careful I didn't give him a chance to sue me for libel. There weren't any witnesses. He could say anything he liked—"

"Will you tell me his name?"

"Parnock."

"Thanks." Simon made a note on the back of an envelope. "Now will you do something else for me?"

"What is it?"

"Promise not to do anything drastic before Tuesday. I'm going away for the week-end, but Parnock won't be able to do anything very villainous either. I may be able to do something for you—I have quite a way with me," said the Saint bashfully.

This was on a Friday—a date that Simon Templar had never been superstitious about. He was on his way to Burnham for a week-end's bumping about in a ten-ton yawl, and the fact that Mr. Inwood's misadventure had made him miss his train was a small fee for introduction to Mr. Parnock. He caught a later train with plenty of time to spare; but before he left the elderly chemist he obtained an address and telephone number.

He had another surprise the next morning, for he was searching for a certain penny to convince his incredulous host and owner of the yawl about a statement he had made at the breakfast table, and he couldn't find it.

"You must have spent it," said Patricia.

"I know I haven't," said the Saint. "I paid our fares yesterday afternoon out of a pound note; and I bought a magazine for a bob—I didn't spend any coppers."

"What about those drinks at the pub last night?" said the host and owner, who was Monty Hayward.

"We had one round each, at two-and-a-tanner a time. I changed a ten-bob note for my whack."

Monty shrugged.

"I expect you put it in a slot machine to look at rude pictures," he said.

Simon found his bottle and silvered another penny for demonstration purposes. It was left on a shelf in the saloon, and Simon thought no more about it until the following morning. He was looking for a box of matches after breakfast when he came across it; and the sight of it made him scratch his head, for there was not a trace of silver on it.

"Is anyone being funny?" he demanded; and after he had explained himself there was a chorus of denial.

"Well, that's damned odd," said the Saint.

He plated a third penny on the spot, and put it away in his pocket with a piece of paper wrapped round it. He took it out at six o'clock that evening, and the plating had disappeared.

"Would you mind putting me ashore at Southend, Monty?" he said. "I've got some business I must do in London."

He saw Inwood that night; and after the chemist had sniffed at the bottle and tested its remarkable properties he told the Saint certain things which had been omitted from the syllabus of Simon Templar's variegated education. Simon paced the shabby inventor's shabby little lodging for nearly an hour afterwards, and went back to his own flat in a spirit of definite optimism.

At eleven o'clock the next morning he presented himself at Mr. Parnock's office in the Strand. The inscription on the frosted-glass panel of the door informed him that Mr. Parnock's baptismal name was Augustus, and an inspection of Mr. Parnock himself showed that there had been at least one parent with a commendable prescience in the matter of names. Mr. Parnock was so august a personage that it was impossible to think of anyone abbreviating him to "Gus." He was a large and very smooth man, with a smooth convex face and smooth clothes and smooth hair and a smooth voice—except for the voice, he reminded Simon of a well-groomed seal.

"Well, Mr.—er—"

"Smith," said the Saint—he was wearing a brown tweed coat and creaseless grey flannel trousers, and he looked agitated. "Mr. Parnock—I saw your advertisement in the *Inventor's Weekly*—is it true that you help inventors?"

"I'm always ready to give any assistance I can, Mr. Smith," said Mr. Parnock smoothly. "Won't you sit down?"

The Saint sat down.

"It's like this, Mr. Parnock. I've invented a method of chromium plating in one process—you probably know that at present they have to nickel plate first. And my method's about fifty per cent cheaper than anything they've discovered up to the present. It's done by simple immersion, according to a special formula." The Saint ruffled his hair nervously. "I know you'll think it's just another of these crazy schemes that you must be turning down every day, but—Look here, will this convince you?"

He produced a letter and handed it across the desk. It bore the heading of one of the largest motor-car manufacturers in the country, and it was signed with the name of the managing director. Mr. Parnock was not to know that among Simon Templar's most valued possessions were a portfolio containing samples of notepaper and envelopes from every important firm in the kingdom, surreptitiously acquired at considerable trouble and expense, and an autograph album in which could be found the signatures of nearly every Captain of Industry in Europe. The letter regretted that Mr. Smith did not consider five thousand pounds a suitable offer for the rights in his invention, and invited him to lunch with the writer on the following Friday in the hope of coming to an agreement.

"You seem to be a very fortunate young man," said Mr. Parnock almost enviously, returning the document. "I take it that the firm has already tested your discovery?"

"It doesn't need any tests," said the Saint. "I'll show it to you now."

He produced his little brown bottle, and borrowed Mr. Parnock's brass ashtray for the experiment. Before Mr. Parnock's eyes it was silvered all over in a few seconds.

"This bottle of stuff cost about a penny," said the Saint; and Mr. Parnock was amazed.

"I don't wonder you refused five thousand for it, Mr. Smith," he said, as smoothly as he could. "Now, if you had come to me in the first place and allowed me to act as your agent—"

"I want you to do even more than that."

Mr. Parnock's eyebrows moved smoothly upwards for about an eighth of an inch.

"Between ourselves," said the Saint bluntly, "I'm in the hell of a mess."

The faintest gleam of expression flitted across Mr. Parnock's smooth and fish-like eyes, and gave way to a gaze of expectant sympathy.

"Anything you wanted to tell me, Mr. Smith, would of course be treated confidentially."

"I've been gambling—living beyond my means —doing all sorts of silly things. You can see for yourself that I'm pretty young. I suppose I ought to have known better. . . . I've stopped all that now, but—two months ago I tried to get out of the mess. I gave a dud cheque. I tried to stay in hiding—I was working on this invention, and I knew I'd be able to pay everyone when I'd got it finished. But they found me last Friday. They've been pretty decent, in a way. They gave me till Wednesday noon to find the money. Otherwise—"

The Saint's voice broke, and he averted his face despairingly.

Mr. Parnock gazed down at the silvered ashtray, then at the letter which was still spread open on his blotter, and rubbed his smooth chin thoughtfully. He cleared his throat.

"Come, come!" he said paternally. "It isn't as bad as all that. With an asset like this invention of yours, you ought to have nothing to worry about."

"I told them about it. They were just polite. Wednesday noon or nothing, and hard cash—no promises. I suppose they're right. But it's all so wrong! It's unjust!"

Simon stood up and shook his fists frantically at the ceiling; and Mr. Parnock coughed.

"Perhaps I could help," he suggested.

The Saint shook his head.

"That's what I came to see you about. It was just a desperate idea. I haven't got any friends who'd listen to me—I owe them all too much money. But now I've told you all about it it all sounds so feeble and unconvincing. I wonder you don't send for the police right away."

He shrugged, and picked up his hat. Mr. Parnock, a cumbersome man, moved rather hastily to take it away from him and pat him soothingly on the shoulder.

"My dear old chap, you mustn't say things like that. Now let's see what we can do for you. Sit down." He pressed the Saint back towards his chair. "Sit down, sit down. We can soon put this right. What's the value of this cheque?"

"A thousand pounds," said the Saint listlessly.

"But it might as well be a million for all the chance I've got of finding the money."

"Fortunately that's an exaggeration," said Mr. Parnock cheerfully. "Now this invention of yours —have you patented it?"

Simon snorted harshly.

"What with? I haven't had a shilling to call my own for weeks. I had to offer it to those people just as it stood, and trust them to give me a square deal."

Mr. Parnock chuckled with great affability. He opened a drawer and took out his cheque-book.

"A thousand pounds, Mr. Smith? And I expect you could do with a bit over for your expenses. Say twenty pounds. . . . One thousand and twenty pounds." He inscribed the figures with a flourish. "I'll leave the cheque open so that you can go round to the bank and cash it at once. That'll take a load off your mind, won't it?"

"But how do you know you'll ever see it back, Mr. Parnock?"

Mr. Parnock appeared to ponder the point, but the appearance was illusory.

"Well, suppose you left me a copy of your formula? That'd be good enough security for me. Of course, I expect you'll let me act as your agent, so I'm not really running any risk. But just as a formality. . . ."

The Saint reached for a piece of paper.

"Do you know anything about chemistry?"

"Nothing at all," confessed Mr. Parnock. "But I have a friend who understands these things."

Simon wrote it on the paper and passed it over. Mr. Parnock studied it wisely, as he would have studied a Greek text.

$$Cu + Hg + HNO_3 + Bf = CuHgNO_3 + H_2O + NO_2$$

"Aha!" said Mr. Parnock intelligently. He folded the paper and stowed it away in his pocket-book, and stood up with his smooth, fruity chuckle. "Well, Mr. Smith, you run along now and attend to your business, and come and have lunch with me on Thursday, and let's see what we can do about your invention."

"I can't tell you how grateful I am to you, Mr. Parnock," said the Saint almost tearfully, as he shook the patent agent's smooth, fat hand; but for once he was speaking nothing but the truth.

He went down to see Inwood again later that afternoon. He had one thousand pounds with him, in crisp new Bank of England notes; and the shabby old chemist's gratitude was worth all his trouble. Inwood swallowed several times, and blinked at the money dazedly.

"I couldn't possibly take it," he said.

"Of course you could, uncle," said the Saint. "And you will. It's only a fair price for your invention. Just do one thing for me in return."

"I'd do anything you asked me to," said the inventor.

"Then never forget," said Simon deliberately, "that I was with you the whole of this morning—from half-past ten till one o'clock. That might be rather important." Simon lighted a cigarette and stretched himself luxuriously in his chair. "And when you've got that thoroughly settled into your memory, let us try to imagine what Augustus Parnock is doing right now."

It was at that precise moment, as a matter of history, that Mr. Augustus Parnock and his friend who understood those things were staring at a brass ashtray on which no vestige of plating was visible.

"What's the joke, Gus?" demanded Mr. Parnock's friend at length.

"I tell you it isn't a joke!" yelped Mr. Parnock. "That ashtray was perfectly plated all over when I put it in my pocket at lunch-time. The fellow gave me his formula and everything. Look—here it is!"

The friend who understood those things studied the scrap of paper, and dabbed a stained forefinger on the various items.

"Cu is copper," he said. "Hg is mercury, and HNO_3 is nitric acid. What it means is that you dissolve a little mercury in some weak nitric acid; and when you put it on copper the nitric acid eats a little of the copper, and the mercury forms an amalgam. $CuHgNO_3$ is the amalgam—it'd have a silvery look which might make you think the thing had been plated. The other constituents resolved themselves into H_2O, which is water, and NO_2, which is a gas. Any schoolboy could have told you that. Of course, the nitric acid goes on eating, and after a time it destroys the amalgam and the thing looks like copper again. That's all there is to it."

"But what about the Bf?" asked Mr. Parnock querulously.

His friend shrugged.

"I can't make that out at all—it isn't any chemical symbol," he said; but it dawned on Mr. Parnock later.

THE UNUSUAL ENDING

Simon Templar buttered a thin slice of toast and crunched happily.

"I have been going into our accounts," he said, "and the result of the investigation will amaze you."

It was half-past eleven; and he had just finished breakfast. Breakfast with him was always a sober meal, to be eaten with a proper respect for the gastronomic virtues of grilled bacon and whatever delicasy was mated with it. On this morning it had been mushrooms, a dish that had its own unapproachable place in the Saint's ideal of a day's beginning; and he had dealt with them slowly and lusciously, as they deserved, with golden wafers of brown toast on their port side and an open newspaper propped up against the coffee-pot for scanning to starboard. All that had been done with the solemnity of a pleasant rite. And now the last slice of toast was buttered and marmaladed, the last cup of coffee poured out and sugared, the first cigarette lighted and the first deep cloud of smoke inhaled; and the time had come when Simon Templar was wont to touch on weighty matters in a mood of profound contentment.

"What is the result?" asked Patricia.

"Our running expenses have been pretty heavy," said the Saint, "and we haven't denied ourselves much in the way of good things. On the other hand, last year we had a couple of the breaks that only come once in a lifetime, which just helps to show how brilliant we are. Perrigo's illicit diamonds, and dear old Rudolf's crown jewels." The Saint smiled reminiscently. "And this current year's sport and dalliance hasn't been run at a total loss. In fact, old darling, at this very moment we're worth three hundred thousand quid clear of all overhead; and if that isn't something like a record for a life of crime I'll eat my second-best hat. I'm referring, of course," said the Saint fastidiously, "to a life of honest crime. Company promoters and international financiers we don't profess to compete with."

Chief Inspector Claud Eustace Teal, on the same day, reviewed the same subject with less content-ment, which was only natural. Besides, he had the Assistant Commissioner's peculiarly sarcastic and irritating sniff as an *obbligato*.

"I gather," said the Assistant Commissioner, in his precise and acidulated way, "that we are to wait until this man Templar has made himself a million-aire, when presumably he will have no further in-centive to be dishonest."

"I wish I could believe that," said Teal funereal-ly.

He had a definite feeling of injustice about that interview, for on the whole the past twelve months had been exceptionally peaceful. Simon Templar had actually been on the side of the Law in two different cases, whole-heartedly and without much financial profit; and his less lawful activities, during the period with which Teal's report dealt, were really little more than rumours. Undoubtedly the Saint had enriched himself, and done so by methods which would probably have emerged somewhat tattered from the close scrutiny of a jury of moralists; but there had been no official complaints from the afflicted parties—and that, Teal felt, was as much as his responsibility required. Admittedly, the afflicted parties might not have known whom to accuse, or, when they knew, might have thought it better not to complain lest worse befall them; but that was outside Teal's province. His job was to deal in an official manner with officially recognised crimes, and this he had been doing with no small measure of success. The fact that Simon Templar's head, on a charger, had not been included in his list of offerings, however, appeared to rankle with the exacting Commissioner, who sniffed his dissatisfied and exasperating sniff several times more before he allowed Mr. Teal to withdraw from his sanctum.

It was depressing for Mr. Teal, who had been minded to congratulate the Saint, unofficially, on the discretion with which he had lately contrived to avoid those demonstrations of brazen lawlessness which had in the past added so many grey hairs to Teal's thinning tally. In the privacy of his own office, Mr. Teal unwrapped a fresh wafer of chewing-gum and meditated moodily, as he had done before, on the unkindness of a fate that had thrown such a man as Simon Templar across the path of a promising career. It removed nearly all his enthusiasm from the commonplace task of apprehending a fairly commonplace swindler, which was his scheduled duty for that day.

But none of these things could noticeably have saddened Simon Templar, even if he had known about them. Peter Quentin, intruding on the conclusion of the Saint's breakfast shortly afterwards, felt that the question, "Well, Simon, how's life?" was superfluous; but he asked it.

"Life keeps moving," said the Saint. "Another Royal Commission has been appointed, this time to discuss whether open-air restaurants would be likely to lower the moral tone of the nation. Another law has been passed to forbid something or other. A Metropolitan Policeman has won a first prize in the Irish Sweep. And you?"

Peter helped himself to a cigarette, and eyed the Saint's blue silk Cossack pyjamas with the unconscious and unreasonable smugness of a man who has dressed for breakfast and been about for hours.

"I can see that I haven't any real criminal instincts," he remarked. "I get up too early. And what are the initials for?"

Simon glanced down at the monogram embroidered on his breast pocket.

"In case I wake up in the middle of the night and can't remember who I am," he said. "What's new about Julian?"

"He skips to-day," said Peter. "Or perhaps tomorrow. Anyway, he's been to the bank already and drawn out more money than I've ever seen before in hard cash. That's why I thought I'd better knock off and tell you."

Mr. Julian Lamantia should be no stranger to us. We have seen him being thrown into the Thames on a rainy night. We have seen him in his

J. L. Investment Bureau, contributing to the capital required for buying a completely worthless block of shares.

If Mr. Lamantia had restricted himself to such enterprises as those in which the Saint's attention had first been directed towards him, we might still have been able to speak of him in the present tense. He had, in his prime, been one of the astutest skimmers of the Law of his generation. Unfortunately for him he became greedy, as other men like him have become before; and in the current wave of general depression he found that the bucket-shop business was not what it was. His mind turned towards more dangerous but more profitable fields.

Out through the post, under the heading of the J. L. Investment Bureau, went many thousands of beautifully printed pamphlets, in which were described the enormous profit that could be made on large short-term loans. The general public, said the pamphlet, was not in a position to supply the sums required for these loans, and therefore all these colossal profits, gravitated exclusively into the pockets of a small circle of wealthy financial houses. Nevertheless, explained the pamphlet, as the hymnbook had done before it, little drops of water, little grains of sand, make the tiddly-tum-tum and the tumty-tum. It was accordingly mooted that, under the auspices of the J. L. Investment Bureau, sums of from £ 5 to £ 100 might be raised from private investors and in the aggregate provide the means for making these great short-term loans, of which the profits would be generously and proportionately shared with the investors.

It was a scheme which, in one form or another, is as old as some of the younger hills and as perennially fruitful as a parson's wife. Helped on by the literary gifts of Mr. Lamantia, it proceeded in this reincarnation as well as it always will. From the first issue of circulars thousands of pounds poured in, and after a very brief interval the first monthly dividend was announced at ten per cent—and paid. In another thirty days the second month's dividend was announced at fifteen per cent—and paid. The third month's dividend was twenty per cent— "which," a second issue of circulars hoped, "should remain as a regular working profit"—and the money was pouring in almost as fast as it could be banked. The original investors increased their investments frantically and told their friends, who also subscribed and spread the good news. The dividends, of course, were paid straight out of the investor's own capital and the new subscriptions that were continually flowing in; but any suspicion of such low duplicity was, as usual, far from the minds of the innocent suckers who in a few months built up Mr. Julian Lamantia's bank balance to the amazing total of £85,000.

Like all get-rich-quick schemes, it had its inevitable breaking-point, and this Mr. Lamantia knew. "Clean up while it lasts and get out," is the only possible motto for its promoter; but a certain fatal doubt has often existed about how long it may safely be expected to last. Mr. Lamantia thought that he had gauged the duration to a nicety. On this morning whose events we have been following, Mr. Lamantia drew out his balance from the bank, packed it neatly in a small leather bag, and called back at his office. Perhaps that was a foolish thing to do, but his new secretary was a very beautiful girl. It was Saturday, and the weekend would give him a long start on his getaway. He had a new passport in another name, his passage was booked from Southampton, his luggage was packed and gone, his moustache ready for mowing: only one thing more was needed.

"Well," he said bluntly, "have you made up your mind?"

"I should like to come, Mr. Lamantia."

"Julian," said Mr. Lamantia attractively, "will do. Haven't you got a first name—Miss Allfield?"

"Kathleen," said the girl, with a smile. "Usually Kate."

The name meant nothing to Mr. Lamantia, who did his best to hold aloof from ordinary criminal circles. He said he preferred Kathleen.

"When do you go?" she asked.

"This afternoon."

"But you told me—"

"I've had to change my plans. I had a cable from Buenos Aires at my hotel this morning—I must get there as soon as I possibly can."

He had not taken her into his confidence. That could be done later, by delicate and tactful stages, if he felt like prolonging the liaison. His projected journey to South America had been discussed as a purely business affair, in connection with vague talk of a gigantic loan to the Argentine National Railways.

"It would be a wonderful trip for you," he said. "New places, new people, no end of new entertainments. Never mind about a lot of luggage. You can go home now and pack everything you want to take from London, and anything else you need you can buy at Lisbon."

She hesitated for a few moments, and then

turned her deep brown eyes back to him.

"All right."

His gaze stripped her in quiet elation, but he did not try to make love to her. There would be plenty of time for that. He put on his hat again and went home to finish the last items of his packing; and when he had gone Kate Allfield picked up his private telephone and called the Saint's flat.

Peter Quentin answered it, and returned after a few minutes to the bathroom, where the Saint was washing his razor.

"It's to-day," he said. "The boat train leaves at two-thirty, and Kate is supposed to be meeting Julian for lunch at the Savoy first. Kate," said Peter reflectively, unaware that the same thought had struck Mr. Lamantia, "isn't nearly so nice as Kathleen."

Simon turned off the taps that were filling his bath, threw off his pyjamas, and sank into the warm water.

"You have been seeing quite a lot of her lately, haven't you?" he murmured.

"Only on business," said Peter, with unnecessary clearness. "After she put us on to this stunt of Julians, and volunteered to do the inside stand—"

"And the new vocabulary, Peter? Did you get that out of a book?"

The Saint's mocking blue eyes swerved down from the ceiling and aimed directly at the other's face. Peter went red.

"I think I did get it from her," he said. "But that's nothing."

Simon picked up the soap and lathered his legs thoughtfully.

"In the preliminary palaver of that Star of Mandalay affair, she told me she was about ready to retire."

"I don't see why she shouldn't," said Peter, judicially.

"I don't see why anyone shouldn't retire," said the Saint, "when they've made a useful pile. Look at you."

"Why look at me?"

"You've done pretty well since we teamed up. About fifteen thousand quid, I make it."

These chronicles have only attempted to record a few incidents in the Saint's career that were distinguished by some odd twist of luck or circumstance or ingenuity. His crimes were always legion; and it is often hard for the historian to select the exploits which seem most worthy of commemoration.

"I owe you a lot," said Peter.

"Brickdust," said the Saint tersely.

He spread the lather over his arms and chest and shoulders, and submerged himself again. Then he said:

"Peter, I let you come in with me because you wanted to and you'd lost your job and you had to live somehow. Now you've got fifteen thousand quid, nine hundred a year or more if you invest it skilfully, and you don't need a job. You don't need to run to seed in an office. You're not rich, but you can have all the fun in the world. You can go anywhere, do almost anything you like within reason. If I may talk to you like an uncle—don't be the pitcher that goes once too often to the well."

"You've never stopped," said Peter.

The Saint grinned.

"I never could. While I'm strong and alive, I've got to go on. When I stop crashing about the world and raising hell, I might as well die. Excitement, danger, living on tip-toe all the time—that's what life means to me. But it isn't the same for you."

"What will you do now?"

"I'm blowed if I know. I think I shall travel south, and put my trust in the Lord. Something's sure to happen. Something always *does* happen, if you go out and challenge it. Adventure never comes. You have to lug it in by the ears. You might settle down in a nice house in England for fifty years, and nothing would ever happen. A few people would die, a few people would get married, they might change over from auction to contract or back again, the man next door might run off with his wife's sister and the grocer's assistant might run off with the till—that's all. But you won't find adventure unless you look for it, and that means living dangerously. Sometimes when I hear fools complaining that life is dull, I want to advise them to knock their bank manager on the head and grab a handful of money and run. After a fortnight, if they could keep running that long, they'd know what life meant. . . . I expect I shall do something like that, and the chase will start all over again. But somewhere in the south it will be, Peter. Do you know, when I woke up this morning it was cold enough for me to see my breath going up like steam, and when that happens I feel the old call of long days and sunshine and blue skies."

He stood up, twitched out the plug, and turned the tap of the cold shower. For a few seconds he stood under it, letting it stream down over him and laughing at the stinging brunt of it, rubbing the water over his arms and thighs and chest in a sheer pagan delight of hardiness; and then he climbed out and reached for a towel and a cigarette, and his wet hand smote Peter between the shoulderblades.

"And I feel like a million dollars on it," he said. "Come on—let's go and be rude to Julian!"

In a surprisingly short space of time he was dressed, immaculate and debonair as ever, and they walked up Piccadilly together.

"No alibi?" asked Peter.

"Why bother?" smiled the Saint. "If anything could possibly go wrong, Julian would have a swell job trying to explain exactly why he had the entire capital of the firm in a bag in his room, with a one-way passage booked to Buenos Aires—and I don't think he'd take it on."

He had a faultless sense of time, and Kate All-field had also learned that in their profession punctuality may be more precious than many alibis. She had just paid off her taxi when they arrived at the Savoy; and Simon could understand the foolishness of Julian Lamantia no less than the foolishness of Peter Quentin. He had always thought her lovely, even at that first meeting on Croydon aerodrome when he had only just discovered the hypnotic powers of her cigarettes in time; and the affair of the Star of Mandalay had shown him something else about her that he saluted in his own way. But it was Peter Quentin's hand that she touched first; and Simon knew that with this adventure one more adventurer came to an end.

They went in together, and Peter and Simon stood aside while the girl approached the hall porter and had her name telephoned up to Mr. Lamantia's room. The reply came back, as they had expected, that she was to be shown up; and the two men strolled along and joined her quite naturally as she was escorted to the lift.

They got out on the third floor, and she stopped the pageboy who accompanied them with a smile.

"I know the way," she said.

Simon slipped a half-crown into the midget's hand, and they brushed past him. In a few yards they had the corridor to themselves.

"You might wander downstairs and drift out, Kathleen," said the Saint. "Go to the Carlton. We'll join you there in about half an hour."

She nodded; and Peter's fingers slipped away from hers as they passed on.

They reached Mr. Lamantia's room, and Simon lifted his hand and knocked.

Using our renowned gifts of vivid description, it would be possible for us to dilate upon Mr. Lamantia's emotions at great length; but we have not the time. Neither, in point of fact, had Mr. Lamantia. He suffered more or less what a happy bonfire would suffer if the bottom fell out of a reservoir suspended directly over it. With eighty-five thousand pounds in bank-notes of small denominations in his bag, an express service to the tall timber mapped out in front of him, and his aesthetic soul ripe with the remembered beauty and tacit acquiescence of the most beautiful girl he had ever seen, he opened his door with the vision of her face rising before his eyes, and saw the vision smashed into a whirling kaleidoscope of fragments that came together again as the lean smiling figure of the man who had once come striding through the wet night to drag him out of his car and immerse him in the Thames. His eyes bulged and his jaw dropped; and then the lean figure's hand pushed him kindly but firmly backwards and followed him on into the room, and Peter Quentin closed the door behind them and put his back to it.

"Well, Julian," said the Saint breezily, "how are all the little stocks and shares to-day?"

A tinge of colour squeezed slowly back into Mr. Lamantia's ashen face. When he had first seen the figures of men outside his door he had had one dreadful instant of the fear that perhaps after all he had left his retirement too late.

"How did you get up here?" he stammered.

"We flew," said the Saint affably.

Suddenly his left fist shot over with the whole weight of his shoulder behind it. The upper knuckles came on the line of Mr. Lamantia's twitching mouth, the lower knuckles on the point of his jaw-bone, clean and crisp in the horizontal centre of his face; and Mr. Lamantia had a hazy feeling that his brain had been knocked off its moorings and was revolving slowly and painfully inside his skull. When it had settled down again to a rhythmic but stationary singing, he became aware that the automatic which he had been trying to pull from his hip pocket was gone.

"Tie him up, Peter," said the Saint calmly.

Peter Quentin came off the door and produced a coil of stout cord from under his coat. Mr. Lamantia went down fighting, but Peter's muscular handling rapidly reduced him to mere verbal protest, which was largely biological in tone.

"I'll get you for this, you swine," was his only printable comment.

"And gag him," said the Saint.

The process was satisfactorily completed under the Saint's expert supervision. Simon had found Mr. Lamantia's cigar-case; and while the knots were being tested he talked and smoked.

"I notice that the welkin hasn't rung with your shrieks for help, Julian. Can it be that you have something on your conscience? . . . I'm sorry about all these formalities, but we don't really want a disturbance, and in the heat of the moment you might have been tempted to do something rash which we should all regret. The staff are sure to find you in a year or two, and then you can explain that some pals did this on you for a joke. I'm sure you'll decide that's the best story to tell, but you need a little time to think it over."

He strolled round the room examining the items of Mr. Lamantia's baggage, and eventually chose the smallest bag.

"Is this the one, Peter?"

"That's it."

Simon turned the lock with an instrument he had in his pocket, and glanced inside. The notes were there, in thick bundles, exactly as they had been passed across the counter of the bank. With a sigh of righteous satisfaction the Saint closed the attaché case again and picked it up.

"Let's go."

He bowed politely to the speechless man on the bed, replaced the excellent cigar between his teeth, and sauntered to the door. Without a care in the world he opened it—and looked straight into the face of Chief Inspector Claud Eustace Teal.

If there had been any competition for grades of paralysis in that doorway, it would have been a thankless task for the judge. Mr. Lamantia had already given his own rendering of a man being kicked in the mid-section by an invisible mule; and now for two or three strung seconds Simon Templar and Chief Inspector Teal gazed at each other in an equally cataleptic immobility. Out in the great world around them, ordinary policemen scurried innocently about their beats, the London traffic dashed hither and thither at a rate of hundreds of yards an hour, the surface of the earth was rotating at five hundred miles every half-hour, whizzing round the sun at seventy-six miles a minute, and tearing through space with the rest of the solar system at over twelve miles per second; but in the midst of all this bustle of cosmic activity those two historic antagonists stared at each other across a yard of empty air without the movement of a muscle.

On Mr. Teal's rubicund features showed no visible emotion beyond the isolated, slow, incredulous expansion of his eyes: the Saint's tanned face was debonairly impassive: but behind the Saint's steady blue eyes his brain was covering ground at a speed that it had already been required to make before.

Once before, and once only, in Simon's hectic career, Teal had caught him red-handed; but then there had been a perfect alibi prepared, a grim challenge ready, and a clear getaway in the offing. At other times, of course, there had been close calls, but they had also been anticipated and legislated for in advance. And, with that alibi or getaway at hand, events had taken their natural course. Teal had been baited, defied, dared, punched in the tummy, or pulled by the nose: those were the rich rewards of foresight. But there was none of that now.

And the Saint smiled.

Teal's right hand was still poised in mid-air,

raised for the official peremptory knock that he had been about to deliver when the door opened so astonishingly in front of him: he might have forgotten its existence. But the Saint reached out and drew it down and shook it, with that incomparable Saintly smile lighting his face again with as gay a carelessness as it had ever held.

"Come in, Claud," he said. "You're just in time."

And with that breaking of the silence Teal came back to earth with a jolt that closed his mouth almost with a snap. He advanced solidly into the room, and another burly man in plain clothes who was with him followed him in. They took in the scene in a couple of purposeful glances.

"Well?"

The interrogation broke from the detective's mouth with a curt bluntness that was as self-explanatory as a cannon-ball. The Saint's eyebrows flickered.

"This," he murmured, with the air of a Cook's guide conducting a tour, "is Mr. Julian Lamantia, who recently revived the ancient game of inviting suckers to—"

"I know all that," said Teal thuddingly. "That's what I came here about. What I want to know is why you're here."

Simon's brow puckered.

"But did you really know all about it? Why, I thought I was doing you a good turn. In the course of my private and philanthropic investigations I happened to learn that the affairs of Julian were not all that they might be, so in order to protect his clients without risking a libel action I decided to have him watched. And this very morning my energetic agents informed me that he had drawn all the J. L. Investment Bureau's capital out of the bank and was preparing to skip with the simoleons —I mean abscond with the cash."

"Go on," said Teal dourly. "It sounds interesting."

The Saint hitched one leg on to the table, and drew appreciatively on Mr. Lamantia's cigar.

"It is interesting, Claud. We also learned that Julian was catching a boat train at two-thirty, so our time was limited. The only thing seemed to be for us to toddle along and grab him before he slipped away, and phone you to come round and collect him as soon as we had him trussed. I admit it may have been a bit rash of us to take the law into our own hands like that; but you must have a spot of excitement now and again in these dull days, and we were thinking of nothing but the public weal."

"And what have you got in that bag?"

"This?" Simon glanced down. "This contains the aforesaid simoleons, or mazuma. We were going to take it downstairs and ask the manager to stow it away in his safe till you arrived."

Mr. Teal took the bag from the Saint's hand and opened it. He sniffed, reminding himself of the Assistant Commissioner.

"That's a great story," he said.

"It's a swell story," said the Saint quietly. "And it'll keep the Home Office guessing for a while. Remember that I'm a reformed character now, so far as the public is concerned, and any nasty suspicions you may have are like the flowers that bloom in the spring. They have nothing to do with the case. My reputation is as pure as the driven snow.

Perhaps, as I admitted, we have been rash. The magistrate might rebuke me. He might even be rude." The Saint sighed. "Well, Claud, if you feel you must expose me to that tragic humiliation—if you must let the newspapers tell of the magistrate's severe criticism—"

"I don't want to hear any more of that," barked the detective.

"Just a word-picture," explained the Saint apologetically.

Teal bit down forcefully on his chewing-gum. He knew that the Saint was right—knew that the last useful word on the subject had been uttered—and the clear blue mocking eyes of the smiling Saint told him that Simon Templar also knew. The knowledge went down into Teal's stomach like gall, but in the days gone by he had learned a certain fatalistic wisdom. And this time, for the first time in their long duel, the honours were fairly even.

"If you're quite satisfied," murmured the Saint persuasively, "Peter and I have a date for lunch with a beautiful lady."

"That's your own business," said Mr. Teal, with all the restraint of which he was capable.

He turned his broad back on them and moved over to the bed, where his assistant was wrestling with the knots that held the empurpled Mr. Lamantia; and Simon winked at Peter Quentin and removed himself from the table. They sauntered unopposed to the door; and from there, without a shadow on his face, Simon turned back for his irrepressibly gay farewell.

"Send my medal along by pcst, Claud," he said.

WATCH FOR THE SIGN OF
THE SAINT

HE WILL BE BACK!